I0822806

Table of Contents

Hornwallace Korlinheiser

A Short Story

Sunlight shining through the window of the day room felt warm against my skin and I sat there, basking in its rays, all the while staring at my hand and wondering when I would move it again. Not that I couldn't move it—I possessed all the physical capacity necessary to lift my hand from the table and do with it as I pleased. I wondered not if I could but rather when I would. Would it be now? Or now? Or would it be later?

And if I lifted my hand, what might prompt me to do so? Perhaps I might get hungry and decide to have a snack. Then I would lift it. Or, I might cease thinking of the topic altogether and simply stand to stretch. But as I stared at my hand, my thoughts moved beyond the obvious and beneath the external to focus on the unstated and understated internal. Perhaps I might, by some random act of my mind set in motion by causes and effects from long ago and imperceptible to me now, decide that a particular moment was the right one. Almost as a matter of happenstance. Perhaps. Or perhaps I might not. Perhaps I might—

"Mr. Dornblat." A familiar voice interrupted my thoughts.

Having heard that voice many times, I recognized it immediately, but it always accompanied an unwelcome intrusion, as it did right then, so I ignored it and continued to focus on my hand and the question I posed to myself of when I might lift it from the tabletop. The proposition was an odd one, for certain. Intriguingly circular in nature, though—me forming the question for myself and waiting to be surprised by the answer I might provide. Only now, with the familiar voice calling to me, I found the suggestion of a new option to consider. Perhaps I might lift my hand from the table to slap the person who spoke, particularly one who referred to me by that infernal name.

"Mr. Dornblat," the voice repeated, in spite of my choice to ignore it. "Time to return to your room."

Mr. Dornblat…

For as long as I can remember, people have called me Mr. Dornblat, or some version of it—often simply Mister. When I was a boy, even my father's friends called me Mr. Dornblat. Never Steven, which was the name my parents gave me when I was born. Just, Mr. Dornblat. And they looked intimidated when they said it, as if they knew something disturbing about me and approached me with suspicion. One or two of them even looked afraid. Especially Mr. Daniels … and that guy from the cabinet shop whom I could never stand to be around and whose name, consequently, I chose never to remember.

The reaction of my father's friends was a curious thing for me. At once both troubling and mysterious, which only served to encourage my imagination and at a very young age I began fabricating stories in my mind to account for their awkwardness. Rather quickly, I convinced myself that I had been an axe-wielding toddler and had hacked my father to pieces—my biological father—and that the man they all knew as my father was merely a stand-in. A look-alike appointed by the authorities to cover for my missing father in order to preserve the illusion to society and themselves that my family and I were normal. That the situation was normal. That nothing untoward ever happened. Especially not with me. So as to preserve the even greater illusion that nothing awful ever involved children. Or the more preposterous myth that they—the adults—were normal, too. It was, after all, the 1950s. A time when everyone and everything was perfectly perfect.

Throughout my childhood, as I continued to fantasize about the nature of the responses I received from my father's friends, my thoughts turned in a different direction and I came to imagine that Father—not being my actual father but the appointed stand-in who looked after me—must have done something terribly wrong and was being punished by being forced to live in close proximity to me, the axe-wielding toddler. And of course, I began to imagine what his transgressions might have been, which took my mind deeper and deeper into the convoluted morass that even then I knew lay at the bottom of my soul.

Imagining all of that was a sordid affair that took place solely within the confines of my mind and an endeavor to which I devoted enormous amounts of time and energy, but it could have been easily avoided if they had merely called me by my name. My proper name. The name my parents had given me at birth. But none of them did. Even my father called me Mister—Little Mister, he used to say when I was a child. Not Steven, or Steve, or even, "Hey, you." I never understood why he and Mother went to the trouble of naming me, then never bothered to use the name.

After enduring the names everyone else gave me, and after noticing that my parents failed to use the name they had officially bestowed upon me, I decided to choose a name for myself, one that I liked, and after some thought settled upon the name Hornwallace Korlinheiser. By then I was in second grade and my classmates thought it was a stupid name. Several of them showed no hesitancy in telling me so to my face, but it was the name I liked and when they persisted in refusing to call me Steve, I became equally obstinate in demanding they call me Hornwallace.

For almost three weeks, I refused to answer the teacher when she addressed me as Steven—it was too late for that name. I had moved on. As a result of my obstinate attitude, I was sent to the principal's office. An event that occurred every day. But I refused to address the principal, too, which he found amusing.

I refused to talk to my friends for the same reason and was the object of their ridicule, especially in the cafeteria where they threw things at me and called me all manner of names, many of them I could not even repeat to Mother, the one person to whom I could tell everything. And then, Benny Smith tried to eat carrots from my plate. Just once, though, because

I doused him with a carton of milk. His parents were at work, which meant they couldn't bring him fresh clothes and he was forced to wear a soured shirt the remainder of the day. I, on the other hand, received an afternoon at home with the housekeeper, free to do as I pleased.

The following day, Father accompanied me to the principal's office and at last I explained the issue about my name, thinking he would help me rectify the situation. Still, it made no difference. No one ever called me Hornwallace and finally I relented and went in the opposite direction, responding to whatever name anyone used. To my surprise, they began calling me Mister, just like my father, which even now is the way I am known by those from earlier in my life who think they are my friends. In truth, I have very few friends. Only acquaintances. A long list of acquaintances. And all of them call me Mister. Everyone except the nurses and orderlies here at Broadmoor where I reside.

The man who spoke to me that day as I sat by the window staring at the back of my hand—the orderly behind the voice—thinks he is my friend, though he persists in calling me Mr. Dornblat, even after a thousand corrections. That's why I call him Homer, though he tells me his name is something else. He doesn't like Homer any more than I like Mr. Dornblat, which makes us even I suppose.

One thing about Homer that I do like is the pants he wears. They're white, like all the other orderlies, but his are tailored nicely with the hem of the legs just touching the tops of his shoes and the seat of his pants fitting snugly across the cheeks of his butt. Not too tight but not baggy like all the other orderlies. He has a nicely rounded butt, too, and evenly proportioned on each side, though you can't really say that to anyone. At least not from one man to another. Start talking to a straight man about a man's butt and he'll categorize you as gay, then he'll never take you seriously about anything else you have to say. Ever. Which is interesting because that kind of prejudice contradicts many of the things they claim to believe. Like, when I was a child and my parents occasionally took me to church, I heard the preacher talk about how God made all things that exist and that all things God created are beautiful. But no one back then would have allowed us to say that a man's butt was beautiful, though not all are, really.

Homer is handsome enough. And the preacher who occasionally visits me is handsome, too, but I can't tell him that. Homer might not mind, but the preacher would think I'm gay. Not that it matters to me what the preacher thinks, or whether I really am gay, but with some people if they think you think you're gay they'll ignore everything else you say, same as if you'd said you were gay. So I don't tell the preacher he has a handsome face, and I certainly don't tell him he has a cute butt. Which makes sense because his butt is flat and not cute at all.

Most of the time when Homer returns me to my room, it's for meals. When I first arrived at Broadmoor I ate meals with the others in the dining room but Morgan Jackson, an idiot who lived on the next hall, kept eating food from my plate. That, of course, brought back memories from my childhood and the anger that went with it. I did my best to remember that he wasn't Benny Smith but finally I could stand it no more. When he reached for my plate the third time, I dumped his plate in his lap. He howled and cried and made a scene until the orderlies escorted him from the room.

That should have been the end of the matter but others who were seated at our table seized the moment as an opportunity to start a food fight, which they very much enjoyed until orderlies attempted to determine blame for the incident. They all pointed to me and said I started whole thing, which wasn't true. I dumped Morgan's plate in his lap, true enough, but did nothing more. The others, however, availed themselves of an opportunity for the kind of pleasure the idiots at Broadmoor enjoy.

After I explained the situation to Homer, he began to watch and soon after they allowed Morgan back in the dining room, Homer caught him in the act of eating my food but did nothing to stop him. A few days later, when Morgan began eating the carrots from my plate for the third time, I stabbed the back of his hand with my fork. Not a light poke either but a genuine stab that inserted the tines all the way in. Someone in the infirmary had to remove the fork with one of their instruments, which I understand required a great deal of effort. Thereafter, I received meals in my room, an arrangement I very much enjoyed. Eating alone was something I'd done since childhood and I found it to be a peaceful experience.

At other times, Homer took me to my room because it was time to take The Pill. I did not like The Pill at all and soon noticed it came in the afternoon, midway between lunch and dinner. When I remembered to remember that fact, I did my best to be somewhere else. They usually found me and made me take it, but I always tried to avoid it—if I remembered. That day, as I sat at the table with the sunlight coming through the window, wondering when I would lift my hand from the tabletop, I had forgotten about The Pill until Homer called for me.

My sister says The Pill makes me more like myself. I say it makes me more like the self she and others wish I would be. The Hornwallace that I am without The Pill is someone they can't manage, manipulate, or understand. Hornwallace without The Pill sees too much, knows too much, understands too much, and that makes everyone uncomfortable—like the way I made my father's friends nervous when I was a boy. People hide things about themselves all the time and they think they're clever, that no one will ever notice, but most aren't that clever and when someone notices the things they've tried to hide, it makes them angry. And when they notice that someone has the capacity for noticing, it makes them nervous. People have been nervous around me all my life.

In truth, no one really minded the way I was without The Pill, except my sister. She's the one who put me in here. Not because the doctors found anything wrong with me, but because she wanted to control the money. All of it. Her part and mine. She couldn't do that without having them put me in here and getting me on The Pill. That's the only way she could manage the money. She had to manage me first. Otherwise, I saw things no one else saw and knew things no one else wanted me to know. It's like what I said earlier about being gay or talking about gay topics. Tell them you saw something that no one can confirm and they'll think you're crazy. Talk to the people that only you see and they'll say you've lost touch with reality.

At first, no one seemed to notice that I saw people no one else saw. When they finally realized it, most were amused by it and when I failed to mention the people I saw, they asked about them. Had I seen the man with the little girl who walked through the woods behind my house every day at noon? Or, did the woman who went for a walk with her dog at two in the morning really wear nothing but a T-shirt and underwear? Everyone tolerated me and some were even amused by the things I said, but then I started talking about the man who came to visit Gemma Mayfield after her husband left for work in the morning and not long after that, the trouble began.

Gemma was in her mid-fifties. Not bad looking but not a young girl either. She was from a little town near Round Rock, and attended St. Edwards University, where she met Tony Mayfield. Tony was a nice guy, though I did not see him often. He came from a family of successful lawyers and by the time I met him he was already a partner in the family firm, a position that seemed to take most of his time. He left the house early in the morning every day except Saturday and didn't get back until after six in the evening, which meant Gemma was at home alone all day. They had no children.

Gemma used to come to my house after Tony went to the office and we had coffee together several mornings each week. I always thought she was interested in more than coffee. I wasn't even interested in having coffee with her, much less anything else, but when someone knocks on your side door in the morning and you're holding a coffee cup when you answer, it's rather difficult not to offer them a cup, too, which I did and then it became a tradition—knock at the door, it's Gemma, cup's on the counter waiting for you. I suppose I could have avoided the whole thing by not answering the door in the first place but she knew I was at home. I was always at home—everyone knew that—so avoiding her by ignoring her knock would have been rude. We were not allowed to be rude.

Coffee in the morning with Gemma went on for a year or two but then one morning she didn't come over and she didn't the next morning, either. So I started watching and that's when I noticed the blue pickup. It was parked on the driveway near the street at first, like a repairman or something, then I saw it around back and that's where it was parked all the time after that. Showed up about nine each morning and stayed until one in the afternoon. The driver was a young guy and by young I mean a lot younger than Gemma, though by no means a minor. He was tall and muscular but in a rawboned way. Angular, not buff. After he started parking his truck behind the house, Gemma didn't come over for coffee anymore.

Nothing much happened about it until one day Mrs. Washington, who lived across the street, saw me when I went out to get the mail and asked me if I had noticed the blue pickup truck at Gemma's house. I didn't want to talk about Gemma or anyone else and certainly not to Mrs. Washington, and for good reason. She repeated everything she ever heard about anyone or anything she'd ever known. I was certain that whatever she knew about me she repeated, too, so I didn't want to tell her anything about anything because I didn't want her mentioning me in connection with whatever she told to whoever she told it. They could think she was a gadfly if that's what she wanted, but not me.

That morning when I went out to get the mail, Mrs. Washington saw me and before I could retreat to the house she was standing right there beside the mailbox. "Mister," she whispered—even she refused to call me by my proper name. "Have you seen that blue pickup next door?"

"Good morning, Mrs. Washington." I spoke as politely as possible. In addition to all the other things that have been said about me, people have often told me I am too abrupt. At times I do not care what others think of me and at times I do. I was in one of the periods of caring and was making a concerted effort to do better with personal interaction, though I had very little of it as a matter of routine, which suited me just fine, but right then I was caring about not being so abrupt. In retrospect, I should have ignored her.

"That truck is over there every day," she said. "The blue one. It's always on the driveway. Have you seen it?"

It wasn't always there—not every day—and the dissonance created by the inaccuracy of her remark compelled me to correct her. "Actually," I said. "It's only there Monday through Friday and only from nine in the morning until one in the afternoon."

"So, you have seen it."

In spite of my attempts at not being abrupt, I did not wish to continue the conversation so I smiled at her and said, "Have a good day, Mrs. Washington."

Then I turned away and started back to the house. And that's all there was to it, but, as things turned out, it was too much.

A week or two later I received a phone call from my sister. My sister hardly ever contacted me unless there was trouble and I should have known her call that morning meant nothing but trouble. She wanted to know why I was spreading malicious gossip about Gemma. I had forgotten that they were friends.

"I've never spread gossip about anyone," I retorted. "Mother did not allow it."

"Mother was the biggest gossip in town."

The arrogance in her voice set me on edge. "Was there a point to this phone call?"

"You should stop talking about Gemma."

"I'm not talking about Gemma."

"You've been spreading stories about her to Mrs. Washington."

"I didn't spread stories to anyone. Mrs. Washington saw me at the mailbox and asked if I had seen the blue pickup truck in Gemma's driveway. I tried to deflect her question but she kept talking and somewhere in the stream of self-important gibberish she said the truck was always there. That wasn't true. It's not always there. And I felt compelled to correct her. So I told her the truck wasn't always there. That it was only there Monday through Friday from nine in the morning until one in the afternoon. And that is absolutely the truth." Then I hung up the phone.

Not long after that, Gemma came to see me and I told her the same thing all over again. She seemed to believe me, but a few days later I noticed my sister's car was parked in her driveway and I remembered they had been roommates at St. Edwards. At first I thought nothing of it, except to note that my sister's car appeared in the driveway shortly after our telephone conversation. Then I noticed that the blue pickup truck stopped coming to the house and instead, my sister's car was parked there every day, Monday through Friday, from about nine in the morning until one in the afternoon. You can draw your own conclusions about what they were doing. I drew mine, but I've never told anyone what I was thinking. My thoughts were unsubstantiated by any facts other than where and when my sister parked her car at Gemma's house, which meant any discussion of it would have been gossip. Our mother didn't allow us to gossip.

For a month or so, nothing else happened. My sister came and went from Gemma's house with great regularity, but never stopped by for a visit with me or even tossed so much as a wave in my direction, though I was never outside during the day, but she knew I often stood near the window when the sunlight was soft enough not to bother me.

Then one day in the spring, Tony came home at noon, which was really early for him and highly unusual. So unusual that I thought something grave must have occurred as he'd never done that before. Turned out, he had planned a round of golf for after lunch that day and had forgotten to take his clubs with him when he left for work that the morning. He came home at noon to get them and that's when things fell apart.

The first indication I had that something was amiss came from the sound of angry voices inside Gemma and Tony's house. Voices so loud and intense that I heard them even with the radio playing in my kitchen.

Shortly thereafter, the voices were followed by the sound of breaking glass and not merely the tinkle of an accidental goblet bursting against the tile floor—Tony and Gemma had terrazzo tile floors in their kitchen. This was the sound of someone repeatedly smashing glass objects with great force deliberately against a hard surface.

The commotion from next door was so alarming that I went to the dining room window to see what might be happening. That's when I saw my sister rushing across the back deck, clothes in hand with only a shirt wrapped around her waist, a scared look on her face. She hurried to her car and dressed from inside but she only got the top on all the way before Tony came down the back steps after her. She locked the doors as he approached and I heard him shouting angrily while she pulled on her skirt.

A landscaping block lay nearby—part of the border of the kitchen garden that no one ever tended. While my sister tried to dress herself, Tony wallowed the block from its place and lifted it above his head as if to smash it against the hood of her car. Before he could do that, though, I heard the car start and my sister backed it to the street with a speed faster than was safe for such a narrow space.

The car bounced over the curb and Tony tossed the landscape block aside, but he stood in the driveway glaring at her as she drove away. As my sister's car topped the hill near the Johnson house and disappeared from sight, Tony turned to go back inside. That's when he looked over at me and flipped me off with a raised middle finger. I did not respond.

Mrs. Washington from across the street later told me that Gemma had been having an affair. "With a woman." The tone of her voice dripped with disapproval. "Ever since the man with the blue pickup stopped coming over," she explained. "His truck left one day and the next day that lady's car appeared." That lady to whom she referred—the object of Gemma's affection—was my sister. Mrs. Washington didn't live across the street from us when we were growing up. She only moved there a few years ago, after our parents were dead and I had the house to myself. That was all she'd ever known. Just me and the house and Gemma next door. She knew nothing of my sister and I did not bother to inform her.

The day Tony came home and found them, Mrs. Washington had been in the yard working in her flowerbed. She heard their angry voices more clearly than did I and thought once about calling the police, but just as she gathered the courage to do so my sister appeared in the driveway. Mrs. Washington was so startled—my sister was, for all intents and purposes, nude and apparently running for her life—that she could only stare, her mouth agape in a slack-jawed expression. When she told me that, I at once regretted looking out the dining room window. The view from the living room, which faced Mrs. Washington's direction, would have allowed me to watch her reaction, which I am certain would have been far more entertaining than what I actually saw.

Two weeks later, the moving vans arrived and then Gemma's house sat empty. No realtor's sign. No tenants. Just empty. The yardman still came to mow the lawn every Tuesday morning. And the tree service kept the trees pruned and the limbs removed. And someone swept off the porch every few months. Otherwise, it was completely unoccupied.

About a month after all of that, my sister started coming around to see me. She showed up unannounced one morning as I was having coffee. By then I'd heard about her taking Gemma as a roommate. My sister lived in a house twice the size of anything she actually needed and had more than ample space to accommodate two or three roommates, though I couldn't imagine anyone actually wanting to live with her, much less share her bed, as apparently Gemma did.

My sister's troubles—being caught up in litigation over Gemma's divorce, as she apparently was—did not surprise me. Her sexual proclivities were well known to most of us from an early age, though not to our parents at first. Then Father discovered her in the attic naked with a classmate during her senior year in high school and there was no denying it after that. She was gay. Not that it mattered to me, then or now.

Father reacted in his predictable manner—he

ranted and fumed for a week or two, then let it drop. Mother simply ignored the matter altogether. And ignored my sister, too.

From my perspective, Gemma and my sister got whatever they wanted and whatever they deserved. I felt bad for Tony, though. He was a nice guy and not bad looking, either. When he and Gemma first moved in next door he used to lay by the pool in the back yard on Saturdays and enjoy the sun. A few times, when he thought no one was watching, he slipped off his swim trunks. I watched him for as long as I could, taking care not to reveal my position by the upstairs window, but could have watched much longer had my eyes tolerated the glare from the sunlight. He really was quite nice to look at. But the light bothered me and so I couldn't stand at the window for long. Which is why I stayed inside and mostly kept the house dark all the time.

When Father was alive, he wanted me outside and, if not, he wanted the draperies open and the house filled with sunlight. He talked all the time, too, and the noise grated against the surface of my brain. Noise bothered me, except for the radio which I kept tuned to public radio broadcasts. I had a radio in every room of the house, all tuned to the same station. The sound of their voices soothed my mind.

Father's voice did not sound like that.

After Father died, the house grew quiet and still and I could set the drapes anyway I liked, which was darker than most would have preferred. I could function that way, though not so much when Mother turned on all of the lights. Those days, when she fluttered about the house in a frenzy, doing this and that and then another, I retreated to my room with the lights off and the curtains drawn, which is how I came to be standing at the window when Tony was sunbathing next door on a Saturday morning, back when he and Gemma were much younger.

So, after Gemma and Tony divorced and Gemma moved in with my sister, my sister started showing up at my house with uncharacteristic regularity. She was never regular. Never on time. Never on schedule. As a child she was always late to dinner and when she was in school she was never on time for class. Father left her at the store more than once because she wasn't at the car when he was ready to leave, which necessitated a trip by Mother to retrieve her, which meant I had to go along, too. Mother was never allowed to go anywhere alone because Father was afraid that she might not remember to return. Not that he was obsessive. Mother's disappearance was a problem that had been made evident more than once, usually following a period of regular medication after which she convinced herself that she was well and no longer needed the pills from the bottle in the cabinet beside the refrigerator.

With my sister's newfound interest in me, she began arriving for a visit in the morning, about the time I was having coffee. Of course, I answered her knock on the side door with a cup in my hand and felt compelled to offer her one, too. After the second time, I just opened the door and gestured toward the kitchen. "Cup's on the counter. Coffee's in the urn." I think she mistook my response—an acknowledgment of the inevitable more than anything else—as a gesture of warmth and a hint that I was pleased to see her. Nothing could have been farther from the truth. I didn't want to see her or have her as a guest in my house and, indeed, felt not the slightest hint of warmth for her. It's just, when someone shows up at your door in the morning and you answer their knock with a cup of coffee in your hand, it's rude not to offer them one, too. Mother never allowed us to be rude. And she didn't allow us to gossip, either, despite what my sister might say about her.

Every visit was the same. She asked how I was doing. Then about some memory of what it was like in the house when we were children. And then she got to the point.

"Did you really see the blue truck on the driveway?"

"Yes," I replied. As I did every time she asked. "Why?"

"Because Gemma isn't sure that ever happened."

"Isn't sure it was there. Or isn't sure I saw it?

"Isn't sure."

"It was there. I saw it. On multiple occasions."

"How do you know?"

"I have eyes that see."

"And Mrs. Washington saw it?"

"You can ask her."

"I did."

"Then you have your answer."

Every day it was the same and I began to think she was crazy, then I realized she wasn't crazy but she wanted me to think I was. That much seemed certain to me. But the thing I was unsure about was why she wanted me to say the truck wasn't there, because that's the direction she was trying to take the conversation. I knew because I had known her all of my life and I had seen this before from her. First, if she could, she would get me to say the truck might not have been there. Then she'd get me to say it wasn't there at all. But why did she want it not to be there?

If the truck wasn't there, the man who drove it wasn't there. And if the man who drove it wasn't there, then whatever happened when he was there didn't happen. I was never in Gemma's house when he was there so I had no idea what actually occurred when he was present. Fantasies about it, but no actual knowledge. But I did know that the truck was parked on the driveway every morning, Monday through Friday, from nine in the morning until one in the afternoon. That was certain. I never budged on knowing it. I never budged on it having happened. I never said the things my sister wanted me to say. She wasn't the first person who tried to gaslight me in some form or another. And I assume from the way things turned out, Mrs. Washington didn't change her story, either.

Then one day, she stopped coming around. The neighbor still walked her dog at night in her underwear with just a t-shirt to cover it. And the man still walked through the woods behind the house with a little girl at his side. But no sister. No Gemma. No blue pickup parked on the driveway.

Eventually, Tony filed for divorce. Rather than settling quickly, Gemma claimed she was entitled to half of everything so they went to court and litigated. Father said lawsuits made everyone miserable and lawsuits taken to trial made all of their friends miserable, too. I was forced to give a deposition in Tony and Gemma's case. But at least I didn't have to appear in court. Things were bad enough without that. Father, by the way, was correct. We all were made miserable by their dispute.

When the subpoena arrived to compel me to testify at a deposition, I was perplexed as to why they wanted me to say anything to anyone about their situation. Most of what I knew I learned from Mrs. Washington across the street. Of a firsthand nature, I only knew what I had seen from the dining room window—the blue pickup truck parked on the driveway and a description of the driver, along with my sister's car parked in the same place and a few details about the day Tony chased her naked from the house. But when I arrived at the appointed time to give my testimony, things became much clearer.

For one, my sister was present and Gemma was not. I knew at once what was happening and what they were trying to do. They were going to attempt in a formal manner what my sister had attempted when she visited me at my house for coffee—to convince me to say the things they wanted me to say, the things they needed me to say, rather than to speak the truth. Father demanded that we always tell the truth. I always complied. My sister did not. She cared little for the truth except for those few occasions when it served her own purposes. Gemma's divorce case was not one of those occasions where the truth could help anyone except Tony.

I also knew that Gemma was not interested in what I had to say. I think she already knew what I would say. She'd had coffee with me, too. And at a time when there were no expectations on her part or mine. She knew from that experience that I would speak plainly and that I would not care what the people in the room thought of me. On that much, she was absolutely correct. One must always speak the truth and speak it plainly. Father demanded it. I was not about to risk the belt over Gemma's situation, even if Father was long since dead. His belt was wide and he swung it hard. Once had been enough for me. And besides, Gemma had no one to blame for her situation except herself, though for certain she was urged along by my sister.

The deposition began innocently enough. Tony's attorney conducted it and he began by asking the usual perfunctory questions about name, address, and the like. Then he moved on to the salient details rather quickly—the blue pickup truck parked on the driveway and the man who drove it; Gemma's car in its place and details I knew about the day Tony chased her from the house. It made me nervous to have my words recorded by a court reporter but Tony's attorney did not challenge my integrity.

When Tony's attorney finished, Gemma's lawyer took his turn. As I said, Gemma was not present for the deposition but my sister was and as soon as the lawyer got hold of me, she started passing him notes and whispering in his ear. As a result, he asked the same sort of questions she had asked me when she came over for coffee. Did I really see the truck? The driver? Was I certain it was my sister's car on the driveway? Or had Mrs. Washington from across the street suggested it to me? Over and over. Trying to get me to say what they wanted me to say to help their case.

After a while everyone in the room except my sister seemed to understand that I was telling the truth and that I was not going to change my version of it to suit her. Even if I had wanted to I couldn't, and I assure you I had not the least desire to do it. But I couldn't change my story, not for her or anyone else, because I had told the truth the first time and the hundredth time and I wasn't about to risk a belting from Father just to say what my sister wanted me to say. As I have noted several times already, I did that once and I wanted nothing to do with it again, even if Father was dead and gone and not coming back. Father required us to always tell the truth. Which I did that day. Many times over.

Tony's lawyer finished with me by mid-morning. Gemma's lawyer droned on and on into the afternoon, asking the same questions over and over. Asking the same thing but in a different way. I answered the same every time, repeating what I'd said earlier and held it together to the end, which I am certain surprised my sister and frustrated her no end. She wanted me to crack. To change my story so they could discredit everything I and all the others had said. To scream and yell and cause a scene. Anything to help their cause. But finally the futility of the effort taxed the patience of even Gemma's lawyer and when we reached three in the afternoon and my sister handed him yet one more note, he brushed her off with a shake of his head, glanced at the court reporter, and said, "We're done with this witness."

My sister slumped in her chair, a sense of defeat evident on her face, but I rose at once and started toward the door, not giving them a chance at even one more go at me. By then, my clothes were too tight and I felt them rubbing against my skin. The light was too bright, too, and I was getting a headache. And it was hot in there.

As I reached the door to the outside my skin began to crawl and I could stand it no more. I ripped off my shirt and walked to my car, naked from the waist up. When I was behind the steering wheel with the door locked and the windows up, I unfastened my belt and unbutton the top of my pants to let the fabric loosen from against me. I hated it when my clothes touched my skin and they had been touching me all day.

At home, I went straight to my room, turned off the lights and drew the drapes, then stripped naked and lay on my bed. Almost immediately I fell into a deep sleep and remained there until sometime later when I awakened to find myself wrapped in the comforter. It was dark outside and I checked my phone to find three days had passed since the day of the deposition. The inbox for my voicemail was full of messages.

After a moment to gather myself, I put on a pair of soft house shorts and the most worn and ragged t-shirt in my drawer, then went downstairs and made a full pot of coffee. It was three in the morning but after all of that sleep I was wide awake. I sat at the kitchen table until the pot was empty, then went to the bathroom.

Later that morning, after the sun was up, I lay on my bed and listened to the voicemails from my phone. All of them were from my sister. In the first one she screamed at me. I deleted it before she finished and went to the next. She screamed at me some more. I deleted that one, also. In the next, she was calm and spoke in clear, cogent sentences. That's when I knew she was drunk.

A month after the deposition, Gemma and Tony's divorce case came to trial. The man in the blue truck was forced to appear before the judge and Tony's lawyer showed him to be Gemma's paramour. Then my sister took the stand and Tony's lawyer proved her to be Gemma's paramour, too. And Gemma lost a fortune. I wasn't there to see it. They didn't call me as a witness and I didn't go anywhere near the courthouse while they were holding the trial.

Mrs. Washington told me about it, though, and from the result I knew they all had one thing in common—they hated me. Gemma, my sister, and the man with the blue pickup truck because I told what they had been up to, which forced them to admit what they had been doing and prevented them from lying, even without me actually appearing in court.

They knew what I had said and what I would say if asked again and had no choice but to own up to what they'd done and who they were. And even though things worked out in his favor, Tony hated me, too, because I didn't say something to him about all that happened when it actually occurred.

Late one night, about two weeks after Tony and Gemma's divorce trial, Julia Bristow, the woman who walked her dog at night wearing nothing but underwear and a t-shirt, came by for a visit. She was a kind woman with a good heart and, in spite of the way she dressed when she walked the dog, was really quite modest. Like me, she did not care to have her clothes touch her skin, which was the reason she dressed the way she did. I only knew what she wore when she walked the dog because city ordinances required pet owners to pick up after their dogs and one night when the dog relieved himself on my lawn, she bent over to gather the droppings in a plastic bag she carried for that purpose. Rather than stoop or squat she leaned down and as her head went lower than her waist the t-shirt she was wearing slid over her torso and gathered against her armpits. That's when I saw what she wore. Or, rather, what she did not.

The night that Julia came for a visit, she had on shorts and the familiar t-shirt with a man's shirt layered over the top, for which I was quite thankful. Talking to her in the attire she normally wore at night would have been a challenge. She was beautiful and comely and my eyes would have wandered to the enticing parts much too easily for polite conversation. I didn't ask how she acquired the shirt.

It was late, perhaps midnight, when I went out to check the mail that night and Julia was coming along the street, but without the dog. I was suspicious of her presence—it was early for her to be out and she was clothed in a presentable fashion—and without the dog—all of which gave me the sense that the moment was less than spontaneous.

Nevertheless, when an attractive woman chats one up on the street at night and you want to go inside—the mosquitoes were terrible just then—one has no choice but to invite her to continue the conversation elsewhere. When I suggested we do that, she readily agreed.

Because of the lateness of the hour, and owing to the similar nature of our schedules, I offered her a cup of coffee which she accepted without hesitation. None had been made since the middle of the afternoon so I put on a fresh pot. We sat at the kitchen table and talked while it brewed. Julia sat with her back to the window.

"I heard from Margaret that Mrs. Washington's family is putting her in a retirement home."

This surprised me. "Really? She was in the yard a few days ago, digging in a flowerbed. She looked fine to me."

"They say she hasn't been the same since she testified at Gemma's trial."

"It affected her that much?"

Julia shrugged. "That's what they say."

"Her family says that?"

"Yes."

"Where do they live?"

"Her daughter lives in Colorado. I think her son is in Brenham."

My eyebrow arched involuntarily. "I didn't know she had a son."

"Neither did I," Julia replied. "But that's what Margaret said."

Margaret was a friend of Julia's who lived on the next street over, behind Mrs. Washington. I knew her only by name, but had never seen her in person, though Julia referred to her every time we spoke.

The coffee was ready and I poured a cup for us,

then returned to my seat across the table and took a sip. As I placed the cup on its saucer I said, "I don't think I've ever seen anyone at Mrs. Washington's house other than her."

Julia nodded. "Neither have I."

"I should go see her," I remarked. "Where did they put her?"

"Somewhere in Colorado." Julia had a sorrowful expression. "Margaret said she's already gone."

That troubled me and I made a pouty face to show my displeasure. "When did they do that?"

"A few days ago."

Then I began to wonder again about Julia's unexpected appearance that night near my mailbox. Was she in league with my sister? Attempting to sway me to a perspective that benefited her? Surely not Julia. She was always so nice to me. And she seemed attentive to detail, too much so to fall victim to my sister.

Julia seemed to notice my apprehension. "That's the reason I came to see you," she said.

A frown wrinkled my forehead. "You intentionally came to see me?"

"I knew you checked your mail at night sometimes and was watching to see when you came out."

"You were waiting for me."

"Yes."

I was both flattered and concerned. Normally, I checked the mail much earlier in the day—Mother insisted we check it as soon as it arrived, which I always did while she was alive. After she died, I began checking it at night because I didn't like going outside during the day, though I did not often wait as late as midnight to get it. That afternoon had been different for me. I started watching a television show through a streaming service, which turned into a binge, and by the time I had caught up with the latest episode for the current season, the hour was quite late. While I was watching the show, Julia was watching for me. I liked that.

At the same time, however, it occurred to me that she had been watching and waiting for me. An intentional act. The act of someone with a purpose. That part left me concerned. She had a purpose. What was it?

"And why were you waiting for me?" I asked.

Julia took a sip of coffee and swallowed it slowly. "Margaret's daughter works in the Wilson Building, downtown. Her office is on the same floor as Wright Martin Wendell. The investment firm."

The financial firm of Wright Martin Wendell was well known to me. After Father died, Mother inherited everything that had been theirs. When Mother died, her estate was divided evenly between me and my sister. Most of it was held in the form of financial assets. A broker at Wright Martin Wendell looked after it for us.

Julia took another sip of coffee before continuing. "Margaret's daughter saw Mrs. Washington's daughter coming from that office the other day."

"The daughters know each other?"

"Yes."

"We live in a small world."

"It gets smaller," Julia said.

"How so?"

"The next day, Mrs. Washington's daughter was up there again."

"Two days in a row?"

"Yes." Julia looked over at me. "This time, she was with Gemma and your sister."

My mouth fell open in a look of surprise, but it was nothing like what I felt inside. "My sister?"

"Yes," Julia said. "Your sister, Gemma, and Mrs. Washington's daughter."

"That makes no sense, unless they're up to something."

"I know."

"And if it involves my sister, that most assuredly is the case."

"I knew you would see it that way."

"Mrs. Washington just testified against Gemma in a case that undoubtedly affects my sister."

"And might affect you."

"You think what they've done to Mrs. Washington portends something dreadful for me?"

"I don't know your sister, except for seeing her once when she came from the car at Gemma's. But from the way you describe her, I thought you ought to know."

I thought for a moment. "If Mrs. Washington's daughter lives in Colorado. And her son lives in Brenham. How did they know her condition had changed after the trial?"

"Someone had to tell them."

"They weren't here for trial, were they?"

"No," Julia answered.

"And I haven't seen anyone at Mrs. Washington's house since the trial. Have you?"

"No."

"And Mrs. Washington wasn't living here when my sister was still at home."

Julia nodded. "Right."

"So, how does my sister know Mrs. Washington's daughter?"

"Through Gemma?"

"Okay," I conceded. "But why would Gemma and my sister be involved with Mrs. Washington's situation?"

"Aren't they together now? Gemma and your sister."

I nodded my head slowly. "You think Gemma merely invited my sister along because she is now her companion?"

"Could have."

"Perhaps she did."

"But you don't think so."

"I think there's more to it than we know."

Julia took another sip of coffee. "It could be that they were simply going and coming from that office at the same time."

"But they were together the second day. Daughter alone on the first day. Daughter with Gemma and my sister on the second."

"Yeah." Julia sighed. "Not much chance that was coincidence."

"My sister doesn't deal in coincidence," I offered. "She has concocted some intrigue."

"But not Gemma?" Julia asked. "She's not part of it?"

"Gemma doesn't think that way," I replied. "You know her at least as well as I do and I think we both know that if she was a person given to subtlety and intrigue, Tony never would have caught her in bed with a lover."

Julia grinned. "You're right about that. She is fully capable of having sex with just about anyone, but not of doing so without getting caught."

When we'd finished the pot of coffee, Julia excused herself and returned home. After she was gone, I went upstairs to the second floor and sat in a straight-backed chair by the window in the front bedroom, from which I could view almost the entire neighborhood. As I sat there for the remainder of the night, I thought about what Julia had said.

Gemma, Mrs. Washington's daughter, and my sister. All of them together, at the office of the financial advisor who administered our parents' estate. It was strange, but it was also clumsy, open, and obvious. Which was the way my sister operated. She and everyone who knew her thought of her as clever. I knew her as obvious, a point that had been proven to me many times in the past and would be again in the days that followed.

Attending to my half of our parents' estate

required periodic trips to the office of our financial advisor at Wright Martin Wendell. In spite of my relationship with my sister and the separate nature of our affairs, she and I still used the same person to manage our business. Louis O'Neill. A broker who happened to be the same person Father and Mother used during the final years of their lives.

A week or two after Julia visited me and we drank coffee at midnight in the kitchen, I paid O'Neill a visit. It was a regularly scheduled appointment to discuss ongoing matters pertaining to my investment accounts, but that day my sister was in O'Neill's office when I arrived. From the way he acted and from the positioning of the chairs near his desk, I was certain he knew in advance that she was going to be there. Which meant regardless of whatever was about to happen, he had already taken her side in the matter.

They began by mentioning that they had heard how I reacted following the deposition I gave in Tony and Gemma's divorce case. "What about it?" I responded.

"You took off your shirt before you even left the building," my sister said. She had an indignant tone in her voice that made it seem as though this was a great surprise to her. Which, of course, it was not. She'd known this was sometimes my reaction to stress since…a long time ago and she had seen it many times before.

I gave her a smart-ass look. "And you know why, too."

"You don't like to feel your clothes touching you." She said it in a mocking tone that belied the ongoing nature of our relationship.

I responded with a condescending tone. "That's nothing new to you, is it?"

"And then you went home and slept for three days straight," she continued.

A frown wrinkled my forehead. "Who told you that?"

"What does it matter?"

"You weren't there," I countered. "You didn't see me. You don't know what I did."

"You were seen arriving at the house that afternoon. After the deposition." She was using her best know-it-all voice. "And then you weren't seen again until three days later."

"Which means?"

"I know you." Her voice was more strident that before. As if I had offended her by challenging her view of the situation. "I know what you were doing. You were doing what you always do."

Clearly, this was no mere meeting, but an intervention. I should have known right then that she was watching the house, but I was angry over being blindsided by her and O'Neill—the one person in the room who was supposed to be on my side, which undoubtedly he was not. "Then if you know me so well, you wouldn't be surprised if I had slept for three days," I snapped. "Would you?"

O'Neill spoke up. "I understand you sometimes see a woman walking past your house at night."

I glared at him. "What of it?"

He had a pained expression. "You've said she walks her dog in her underwear?"

"With a t-shirt over it," I added. "She doesn't care to have her clothes touch her body and there's no one else out at that time of night." As if that explained the situation.

My sister spoke up. "Do you know that no one else on the street has ever seen her?"

"They've never seen her?"

"At night, I mean." She was aggravated at having to correct herself. "And dressed like that."

"I don't doubt it."

"Why is that?" O'Neill asked.

"None of them stays up that late at night."

"And how late is that?"

"Two or three in the morning."

"What about the man who walks through the woods in the afternoon with the little girl," my sister chided. "Tell him about that." She nodded toward O'Neill when she spoke.

"There's not much to tell," I said. "He walks with her through the woods. They come from up by Mrs. Montgomery's house and go down past the Edleberry's."

"Never in the opposite direction?"

"No." I looked over at her. "Why do you ask me these questions? These matters are well known by many. And especially by you."

"That you have talked about them is well known," she snarked. "But would it surprise you to know that none of your neighbors can verify the man and girl even exist? They've never see the man and the girl. They've never seen the woman walking the dog at night in her underwear. They've never seen either of them."

My sister's motives were easily deduced. She only wanted money, power, and sex. Appetites which had driven her every action and thought all of her life. Obviously, she had lived through her share of the money and was now after mine. The only way she could accomplish that goal was to remove me from control of my own affairs, which I was certain she was now orchestrating events to accomplish. But the great unanswered question for me remained, as it had earlier, with O'Neill and his interest in the matter. So I ignored my sister's question and turned to him. "I am well aware of my sister's intentions here." My eyes bore in on him. "But what are yours?"

O'Neill fidgeted nervously in his chair before saying, "I assure you, my only desire is to preserve your well-being." He looked down as he spoke, with his eyes focused on the desktop, and then I knew why he was there.

"And…?"

He looked over at me. "And what?"

"You've not mentioned the real reason you took this meeting."

"Which is?"

"To protect the firm."

He frowned. "What do you mean?"

"I mean, the real reason you're here is to protect Wright Martin Wendell."

"Well." He glanced away. "We do have liabilities in this regard."

"My sister has asserted that I am no longer competent and you take that as notice of a risk to you."

"Perhaps. But I'm not—"

Anger rose inside me but I kept it bottled up. "I

am certain that I need not remind you that, in regard to my investments, you have a fiduciary duty to me. Not to her."

O'Neill leaned back in his chair. "I fully understand my fiduciary responsibilities, which is why I agreed to meet with you on this."

"No," I said, wagging my finger for emphasis. "It is why you agreed to join her in this charade. Why you agreed to blindside me."

Again O'Neill looked away. "I was only interested in your well-being."

"Then tell me something," I responded. "In all of your dealings with me, have I shown the slightest indication that I am not in full control of my faculties?"

"N…no." He spoke in a tentative voice. "None that I have noticed."

"Have I suggested we invest in tulip bulb futures or some equally ludicrous venture?"

"No. Not really."

"In fact," I continued. "All of the investments in my accounts have been made as a choice between options you provided."

"Well…I've done my…"

"When we met, you offered an array of three or four possibilities. Never one. Never a dozen. But always enough so that I didn't have to choose between only two."

"That's—"

"You arranged it that way so that no one could say that I was guided toward any particular investment option by you. And then I made the choice. I determined which among your suggested alternatives I would choose. Isn't that how it worked?"

"Yes." He was sweating. "I believe so."

"Then I must ask, how is it that you think your firm has any exposure to any risk at all in dealing with me? If there is any risk to the firm, it's in the array of choices you presented to me. Is that not true?"

"Well, I don't—"

"Which means the risk to this firm comes from you. Not me." Then I leaned closer to his desk and with my eyes focused on him, but my finger pointed in my sister's direction, I said firmly, "If she touches so much as one cent of my money, I will sue this firm for fraud. And you will be subject to criminal prosecution."

And with that, I left the building. Only this time, I did not take off my shirt or go home and sleep for three days. This time, I went home and prepared myself for what lay ahead because by then I knew what was coming. My sister intended to file a petition with the court to have me declared mentally incapable of managing my own affairs. If successful, I would be placed in an institution and she would be the obvious choice to control my half of the estate.

As I expected, less than a week after the meeting with O'Neill, a soft, round-bellied sheriff's deputy was at my door with papers requiring me to appear in court on a petition filed by my sister to have me declared incompetent. A notice with the papers indicated that because I was not deemed a threat to my own safety, I was allowed to remain free pending the hearing that had been scheduled on the matter. That fact alone seemed to settle the issue there and then—if I was competent to care for myself in the meantime, as the court assumed by allowing me to remain free, I should be held competent in every respect—but the deputy insisted I had to appear in court.

Later that day, I hired an attorney, Porter Fulbright, to represent me. He was tall and young, with short hair and a muscular build that radiated a certain level of physical prowess—a heady, musky blend of desire and desirableness—evident even from beneath the cover of his dark gray business suit. Though, as with Homer and all the others, one cannot say those things aloud. But best of all, Fulbright was not the lawyer who guided us through the settling of Mother's estate. That one led us on a needless journey through the wilderness. Fulbright, I knew, would be fully capable of dealing with the likes of my sister. I could tell it from the look in his clear blue eyes.

From the things discussed during the meeting at O'Neill's office, I knew how the hearing would go. My sister would testify about the things I said about the people I saw. People that she would contend no one had ever been able to verify—the woman who walked her dog at night in her underwear with only a t-shirt to cover it, the man and the little girl who walked through the woods together, and perhaps the presence of the blue truck at Gemma's house. I wasn't sure whether she would raise the issue of the truck, but something Julia said when she visited me that night made me think the topic might come up.

When I explained this to Fulbright, he said, "We'll need to locate those people and get them to testify."

"The woman who walks her dog at night is easy to find. She is my neighbor."

"What about the man who walks through the woods with the little girl?"

"I haven't seen him in a few days and I'm not sure where to find him."

The lawyer looked determined. "We need him."

"Okay," I replied. "I'll see what I can do."

"Did anyone else see the pickup truck at the house next door?"

"Yes," I said. "Mrs. Washington, who lives across the—" And that's when I realized just how serious this situation really was. My sister had maneuvered Mrs. Washington's daughter into placing Mrs. Washington in a retirement home so she would be out of the way when this hearing came up.

Fulbright gave me a nudge. "Is everything all right?"

"Yes." I cleared my throat. "Mrs. Washington is in a retirement home. Her daughter placed her there a week or two ago. I believe the facility is located in Colorado. Margaret, who lives on the next street behind her, can tell you about it. She is friends with the woman who walks her dog at night. You should speak to both of them." Then I gave him Julia's name and address.

Because of his relationship with the court, Fulbright had the hearing on my sister's petition delayed for a week. I used the time to sit at the window in the back bedroom, watching the woods for the man and the little girl. When, after two days, that proved fruitless, I went into the woods myself, hoping to locate them and convince them to come to court and testify on my behalf. As an added measure, I took my cell phone with me to record our conversation and capture an image of them, thinking that if all else failed the images and recording might somehow help my case.

For three days I sat in the woods, night and day, enduring mosquitoes, wildlife, and rain, but caught not a single glimpse of the man or the girl. As a consequence, I arrived at the courthouse for the hearing freshly cleaned but dotted with welts from mosquito bites and really quite famished. Fulbright, it seemed, had no better success with Julia or Margaret.

"I have been unable to locate either of them," he reported.

As I suspected, my sister took the witness stand and testified about all of things I had said that I saw—the man with the little girl, the woman who walked her dog at night in her underwear, and the blue pickup I reported seeing on Gemma's driveway. She was especially distraught over the matter about the blue pickup truck, which she asserted was painful for Gemma in her divorce. Gemma, however, was noticeably absent.

In the absence of other witnesses, I testified on my own behalf and refuted the matters she raised. The judge listened attentively and, although it seemed from what we had been shown that day—me living on my own, hiring an attorney, appearing as required, and my sister with nothing but her bare statement of allegation to support her cause—we had demonstrated my complete sanity, he ordered that I be held in a psychiatric facility for seventy-two hours while an evaluation was conducted. That's how I came to be a resident at Broadmoor.

The hearing was held in the morning and I was transported to Broadmoor straight away. My sister arrived that afternoon, ostensibly to check on my condition. When she appeared in the doorway of my room I shouted for her to leave. She did not do so immediately and I threw a water pitcher at her. I was aiming for her head but she dodged it—the first nimble move of her life—and the pitcher sailed into the hallway. And that's how I came to receive regular doses of benzoquilamine—known to me as The Pill.

So, while I was sitting by the window in the warm sunlight staring at my hand, wondering when

I would move it again, Homer came and got me and wheeled me to my room—even those of us who could walk were moved by the orderlies in wheelchairs. I assumed he was taking me to my room to receive the daily dose of The Pill. As I mentioned earlier, they gave it to me at that time every day. And always when they gave it to me, they took me to my room. I'm not sure why they did that. It was only a small pill and I could have easily swallowed it without any water at all, but they gave me a large glass to drink with it and stood by watching while I downed it all. Which made avoiding The Pill problematic.

The first time they gave it to me I swallowed it without question but then I noticed the way it made me feel and I did not like it. Rather like being myself but with another body wrapped around the outside, as if I had acquired an extra layer to live through. After that first time, I tried hiding The Pill beneath my tongue until the orderly left the room, which prevented me from receiving a full dosage—provided he left the room promptly and I could spit The Pill into the toilet. That method, however, allowed The Pill to partially dissolve and left a bitter taste in my mouth. Then I learned to distract the orderly with a cough during which I dropped The Pill into my opposite hand and placed it in my pocket. That scheme worked best and in the days that followed I perfected it until I could elude detection completely and avoid ingesting even the slightest amount of The Pill.

This subterfuge with The Pill went on much longer than I anticipated. The initial seventy-two hour hold on me was extended by a week, then by two. When Homer wheeled me from the day room as I sat staring at my hand, I had been confined at Broadmoor four weeks and I was beginning to wonder if I ever would be released, if I ever would see my home again, if I ever would sit by the window upstairs and gaze out at the neighborhood. And as I wondered about that, I considered that perhaps I should simply surrender to the inevitability of my circumstances, swallow The Pill, and yield to whatever might come next. Doing so certainly would have been easier than the constant vigilance I attempted to maintain.

But the thought of giving in to them—to my sister, to the Broadmoor staff, to the authorities—left me sad. I had lived in that house all of my life and for much of it I followed the same routine every day. The thought of being forced to live a different way left me hollow inside. As if the part of me at the center would be taken away and a void left in its place. Routine was important to me and maintaining the one I had was even more so. I abhorred change. Newness was not my friend. Constancy, regularity, rhythm, they were my friends. They kept me going and made life manageable for me. Even productive. Change threatened my existence.

Homer guided me down the hall to my room where I expected to see The Pill sitting inside its paper cup resting on the dresser. Instead, I saw Porter Fulbright, my lawyer, standing by the window on the opposite side of the bed. Homer left us and I moved myself from the wheelchair to the upholstered chair in the corner. Fulbright closed the door, propped against the foot of the bed, and then we talked.

"I located Julia," he said. There was a smile on his face when he spoke and I could see that he was satisfied with himself at finding her. She wasn't difficult to find. She lived just up the street from me and was always home. Though she, like me, preferred to sleep in the afternoon and sometimes into the early evening, which occasionally made getting her to the door between lunch and midnight difficult.

"The woman who walks her dog at night in her underwear." I don't know why I referred to her that way. In a third person sort of way. As if I didn't really know her.

"Yes," Fulbright said.

"What did she say?"

"She confirmed everything you said."

I had an expectant look. "And Margaret?"

"I found her, too." He seemed satisfied with that as well. "Right where you said she would be. One street over."

"She told you about Mrs. Washington?"

"Yes. She did." Fulbright still was smiling so I knew he had something else to say.

"And what else did you find?" I asked.

"The man with the little girl."

My eyes opened wider at the mention of this new information. "You found them?"

"Yes." Then he corrected himself. "I found the man."

"What did he say?"

"He said the little girl is his granddaughter. She stayed with him most of the time but in the afternoon she went to stay with a lady who lived a few blocks away. They cut through the woods because it was shorter and because it gave his granddaughter a chance to see some wildlife, which he enjoyed pointing out to her."

The way he described them seemed odd. "You're speaking in the past tense," I noted.

"They did that when the girl was younger," Fulbright said. "About six or seven. She's in college now.

Which explains why you weren't been able to find them before."

Fulbright spoke as if everything were perfectly normal—a witness sought, a witness found—but for me, the news was quite troubling. I had seen the man and the little girl just a few weeks before I went to court. It was hot and sunny and they were walking through the woods. He in a dark gray suit with a hat. She in a summer dress. From the look of it, the dress was made of cotton. The fabric seemed very light. They were talking and smiling and laughing and I could almost hear their voices.

Was it real? Or was I asleep and dreaming? No. I couldn't have been asleep. I saw them through the window of the back bedroom. That's where I sat when I was awake during the daytime. The front windows were for nighttime. But I noticed Fulbright did not find any of what the man said to be troubling at all so I kept my thoughts to myself.

"They will come to court?" I asked.

"Yes," Fulbright said triumphantly. "They will be there."

"And what about the doctors who examined me here?"

"Other than the outburst you had when you arrived, they say you have been incident free and are capable of taking care of yourself."

"Good." I said it with a soft voice that sounded distracted because my thoughts had moved on from the court appearance to the next topic. "Did my sister clean out my investment accounts?"

"No." Fulbright shook his head. "She hasn't touched them."

"You know this for certain?"

"Yes. I checked with your advisor. He didn't talk to me about the details but he said she had not contacted him since the day he met with the two of you."

This left me puzzled. "Then why all of this?" I had a bewildered look on my face and a troubled tone in my voice.

"Apparently," he replied, "she wanted access to your house."

My forehead wrinkled in a frown. "My house?"

"Yes."

"What for?"

"We're not sure. No one has seen her in several weeks."

I thought for a moment. "Several weeks would be about the time I was brought here."

"That's about right." Fulbright nodded. "That's about the last time anyone has seen her."

"Did you search my house?"

"I went over there, but I don't have any way of getting inside. Other than to break open a door. But that seemed a little extreme."

In spite of the way she acted, the news about my sister was troubling and I felt certain I knew where to find her. I was equally certain my keys were still in the pocket of the pants I had been wearing on the day we were in court. Those clothes were hanging in a closet by the bed. As Fulbright continued to talk, I thought of giving him the key to the house and asking him to check the attic. If she was in the house, she was either there or in her old room but I did not expect him to find her alive. There was no reason for me to think that, other than my knowledge of her as my sister, but the sense I had inside was that she was dead.

I kept quiet about it while we discussed our plans for the hearing that was scheduled to occur a few days later. All the while, however, my mind was torn between conflicting thoughts. If my sister was in the place I thought she might be, she would not be alive. Which meant she would not appear in court. If I kept that information to myself and she failed to show, the case against me would evaporate. Or at least be greatly weakened.

On the other hand, if her body was found after the hearing, the authorities might suspect I had something to do with her death, especially if I was the one who reported the discovery. The medical examiner could determine the time of death and it ought to be obvious that she died while I was being held in Broadmoor. Still, I did not feel comfortable being the one to find her and did not wish to trust myself to the medical examiner's call.

And then there was the matter of foul odor. When Mother died, I was away on a trip to Barcelona, one of the few times I left the country. Mrs. Langston, Mother's closest friend, was supposed to check on her daily but she went to San Antonio to see her daughter. Mother's body lay in her bed for ten days until I returned and discovered her. By then, decomposition was well along and the smell was horrible. I noticed it as I came from the car on the driveway beside the house and knew she was not alive. Gemma or Tony or Julia should have noticed it long before then but they didn't. Removing the odor required the services of a professional remediation company and a painting contractor who applied three coats of paint to the walls and ceiling. I even had the floors refinished and, of course, replaced the furniture. Though the furniture didn't matter. It wasn't old or important. We went through the same thing when Father died so nothing in Mother's room predated his death.

Whatever my sister did, she did of her own accord. I had nothing to do with it. And I had the best proof possible of that. I was confined in a psychiatric hospital at the time whatever happened to her might have occurred. But then I became concerned about Gemma. If something happened to my sister—as I suspected—then something might have happened to Gemma, too. Her family might like to know about it sooner rather than later. And for all I knew, she could be alive and languishing in a closet, her body bound and her mouth gagged. My sister was not above doing something like that if she took the notion.

When Fulbright and I finished our discussion about the case and he was preparing to leave I said, "I think you should check my house."

"For your sister?"

"Yes."

"I would be glad to," he said. "But I don't have a key."

I rose from my chair and crossed the room to the closet by the bed, then reached into the pocket of the pants that hung there and took out a key chain. The house key was on a small ring by itself and I removed it, then handed it to him. "This is a key to the back door. My sister's old room is a middle room at the top of the stairs. First room on the left. The windows look out over the driveway."

Fulbright had a puzzled expression. "She lived with you?"

I shook my head. "The house belonged to our parents. It's the place where we grew up."

"Okay."

"If you don't find her in her old room, check the attic."

Fulbright frowned once more. "The attic?"

"She often hid there when she was a child." It was one of her special places. I slept all day to avoid the light. She hid in the attic for the same reason. And for others, as well.

"You think your sister is hiding there now?" he asked.

"If you find her there," I explained. "You will likely find she is no longer alive."

Later that day Homer came again to the day room where I had returned to sit in the sun and continue my thoughts while staring at my hand. With little in the way of explanation, he placed me in a wheelchair and took me to the administrative office where Fulbright was waiting with a deputy sheriff at his side.

The deputy was a young man of Fulbright's

height but with olive skin, dark hair, and even darker eyes. He was not particularly muscular and I judged by his long frame over which there was hardly any fat that he was a runner. There was a tension about him, too, that gave him a no-nonsense air. All business. No variation. Rigid. Which left me suspicious of why he was present.

They guided me to a conference room and the others followed but the deputy stood back when we reached the door. "I'll be out here," he said. Fulbright acknowledged him with a nod and my sense of suspicion grew to a state of apprehension.

Homer pushed me up to the conference table and then turned to leave. I took hold of his hand to stop him but he slipped it away. "You'll be alright, Hornwallace," he said. A tingle ran up my spine at the mention of it. That was the first time he or anyone else at Broadmoor had called me by my chosen name. It was an exhilarating experience but it told me something bad was about to happen.

The door closed as Homer left the room and when he was gone, Fulbright said, "I went to the house like you suggested."

"And you found my sister?"

"She was in the attic," he said.

"And not alive."

"No." Fulbright shook his head. "I'm sorry. She was dead. Had been for several weeks."

"And Gemma?"

"She is alive and well at her home."

I raised an eyebrow. "Alive?"

"Yes."

"That surprises you?"

"A little." I avoided his gaze. "Why is the deputy with you?"

"The court issued an order releasing you temporarily to our custody. They need you to identify your sister's body."

"At the hospital?"

"Yes," he said. "At the morgue."

When Father died I went there with Mother to claim his remains. I did not do that when Mother died as they came to the house and I told them the things they wanted to know about her while they were there. But the mention of the morgue revived a memory of being there with Father. And it revived a memory of the smell as well. The smell of the morgue was a problem for me. Something reminiscent of formaldehyde. The dull putridness of death. The cleaning agents they used. It gave me a headache and I was not looking forward to being there.

From Broadmoor, I rode in the deputy's patrol

car to City Hospital, where the morgue was located. Fulbright followed us in his car, then accompanied us as we made our way across the parking lot to the hospital entrance.

The medical examiner—Robert Pouncey—met us in the hallway just inside the doorway and escorted us to his facility. Pouncey was a middle-aged man. Tall and slender with thinning hair. His sister was in my class at Amherst, though I doubt either of them remembered it. No one at Amherst remembered me, either.

When we reached the morgue, Pouncey took us to the far end of the room where several rows of cooler doors were located. He checked his file for the correct door number, then glanced over at me. "Are you sure you can do this? The body has decayed a good bit. It smells."

"Yes," I replied. "Go ahead." We were there. The smell was everywhere. There was no way out but to get it over with.

Pouncey unlatched the door and drew out a metal rack that held my sister's body. A wave of putrid morbidity gushed out with her. My stomach muscles revolted but I clinched them off and steeled myself against the stench.

The body was covered with a white sheet and

when the rack was fully extended before me, Pouncey lifted the sheet from the head of the corpse. I recognized her immediately but when I didn't speak he said, "Do you know this person?"

"Yes," I answered. "That is her. That is my sister."

Pouncey quickly covered her body with the sheet, then pushed her back inside the cooler and closed the door. As he latched it in place I said, "How did she die?"

"Drug overdose," Pouncey replied. He took a can of air freshener from a cart nearby and sprayed it in the air. The fragrance was almost worse than the smell of my sister's body.

"What kind of drug?" I asked.

Pouncey checked his file again. "Lorazepam and amphetamines," he said.

"I understand she was found in the attic."

"Yes."

"Was there any evidence of those drugs up there?"

Pouncey sorted through several pages of the file. "I was not at the scene but the detective who responded indicated there were two empty pill bottles near the body."

"Do you have those bottles?"

"No." Pouncey shook his head. "You will have to ask the detectives if you want to look at the bottles." Then his eyes opened wide and a sense of realization came over him. "But, there's a photograph in our digital file." He stepped to the far side of the room where a laptop rested on the counter. With a few strokes of the keyboard a file opened and a picture appeared showing two bottles lying on the attic floor.

I studied the image a moment, then pointed. "Can you zoom in on them a little closer?"

"Sure," Pouncey said.

The frame tightened and that's when I noticed one of the bottles was labeled for my sister. The other—the one that contained Lorazepam—was in Gemma's name. "Any estimate of how much my sister took?"

"Based on the date the prescriptions were filled, the contents of her stomach, the blood tests, and the time of death, it appears she ingested about half a bottle of Lorazepam and a full bottle of the amphetamine."

That seemed like a lot to me. "She would have been able to swallow all of that before passing out?"

"Yes."

"She would have needed a drink." My sister couldn't swallow a tiny allergy tablet without something to help her. "Any thoughts on what that might have been?"

Pouncey switched to a different page of the file on his laptop and pointed. "Whiskey," he said. An image of a bottle of Basil Hayden's appeared.

"Bourbon," I corrected, unable to let the discrepancy pass. The bottle of Basil Hayden's in the file wasn't one for whiskey. It was bourbon. A distinction my sister often noted with an odd, nerdy delight.

Pouncey seemed not to understand and responded with a wary nod. "Right."

"You mentioned time of death," I said, moving on. There was no point in explaining myself to him. "How long has she been dead?"

"As best I can determine, she's been dead about three weeks. Maybe four, but not any longer than that."

"Bodies are usually in this shape after three or four weeks?"

"They are if they've been lying in a hot attic."

Dead for about three weeks. Maybe four. The words rolled around in my mind and as they did the implications began to emerge. Based on that estimate, my sister had, indeed, died not long after I was taken to Broadmoor. And from the examiner's description, she died at her own hand. Which meant she had no intention of attending the hearing that would determine my ultimate end. She had no intention of following through with the proceedings she had initiated. She placed me at Broadmoor. Disrupted my life. Turned my world upside down. And intended from the beginning to rest my extrication on my own device.

Yet once again I had been victimized by her. It was nothing new. She had treated me that way all our lives. But this time seemed particularly cruel. She knew how I was and she knew what others thought of me because of it. The judgments they made of me at first sight. Opinions based on the shallowness of their minds but which prevented them from ever knowing me beyond their own myopic stereotypes. Sending me to Broadmoor only validated those opinions and I could hear their voices as plainly as if they were standing in the morgue with us.

"She always said he was crazy. Now we know it for certain."

"Wasn't he in a mental hospital?"

And that idiot Rankin with his arrogant tone, "He sees things and hears things, you know."

True enough, I did see things and hear things. Much of it not seen or heard by anyone else. But that was because I sat by the window at night long after everyone else went to bed and I saw what happened while they were asleep. And in the daytime, whether I was awake or asleep, I heard the sounds they made and recorded all of them automatically in my mind. They, on the other hand, knew nothing because they paid no attention to anything.

Unlike the experiences of others, the noises of life—a passing car, a door opening and closing, a bird flying overhead—were never relegated to contextual clutter for me. Instead, they were always in my ear. The delivery truck, the mail truck, the neighbor's car, the other neighbor's truck, the child pedaling past on a bicycle he received for his eleventh birthday, the voices from the party at which he received it. I heard each of them, separately and distinctly. Yet familiarity did not force the sounds of daily life to recede from the pale of my attention. My brain was never numbed to their existence. On the contrary, it was energized by them. My ears always attentive. My mind always at work. Never resting. Never ceasing to function. All day long. Questions. Answers. Questions. And more answers. Sorting. Resorting. Arranging the information that my senses gathered as I processed the world around me in a constant stream of detail, nuance, rhythm.

After a moment, I returned to the matter at hand

and as I became conscious once again of my surroundings, I noticed that Pouncey and Fulbright were staring at me with a puzzled expression. I had no idea how long I had been standing in their presence without speaking, or even if I had not been speaking, but whatever I had been doing while lost in thought they seemed to take it as rather odd. A reaction I had grown accustomed to in others.

Without explaining myself I thanked Pouncey for his help, then looked over at Fulbright. "Is there anything else to do here?"

"No," he said. "I think we're finished here." He gestured toward the door and we started in that direction, then continued into the hallway. No one said a word as we made our way through the building with only the sound of our shoes clicking against the hard surface of the floor to occupy my mind.

As we neared the exit to the parking lot, the deputy took me by the elbow. "You'll have to come with me," he said.

I glanced over at him. "Any possibility we could go by my sister's house? We need to make sure it is secure."

"We need to—"

Before he could finish, Fulbright turned to me. "Are you in charge of her estate now?"

"I'm not sure." And I really wasn't. I had never seen my sister's will and wasn't certain she even had one. "But until that has been decided, we need to make sure the doors are locked and no one can get inside."

"Do you have a key?"

"No."

"I'll see that the locks are changed," Fulbright offered. "How about that?"

"Okay."

Securing the house wasn't all that I wanted to do, but I was certain the deputy was not going to allow me to visit the property, so I said no more. In spite of his appearance, which was almost as pleasing as Fulbright's, he proved to be a functionary by disposition and rigid by personality. Not the type for viewing situations creatively or for stretching the moment into an opportunity.

Almost on cue, he took me by the elbow again. "Come on," he said. "The court's order was for you to identify the body and go back to Broadmoor. We need to get you back there now." I offered no resistance as we made our way to the patrol car but I was worried, though not for the reasons I implied. Gemma might be living there and if she was I wanted to talk to her about the Lorazepam prescription that bore her name. That, however, like all my other questions, would have to wait.

We returned to Broadmoor without incident and I was wheeled back to my room, though not by Homer. I was just settled in place by the window when dinner arrived. They served all of the meals earlier than I liked, but once on their schedule I adjusted to it well enough. That day I was glad to have the food.

When I had eaten all I wanted I placed the tray in the hall by my door. The sun was still up so I returned to my seat in the chair by the window. Rather than staring at my hand, though, I gazed out at the lawn and thought of the events that had occurred that day, how my sister's death might affect the hearing that was scheduled in my case, and the way it might shape my life beyond that. I was alone now. No parents. No siblings. No offspring. No relatives of any kind from our immediate family. Just me.

For the next two days I kept to myself even more than normal. Each morning, Homer wheeled me to the day room where I sat by the window, but I had no interaction with anyone. There was little need for it. After the incident in the dining hall and after taking all of my subsequent meals in my room, most of the patients I had met when I arrived were either transferred to other facilities or simply forgot who I was.

At noon each day, Homer took me back to my room where I ate lunch. Afterward, I departed from my previous routine and remained there, sitting alone in the chair by the window, staring out at the lawn. Often I did the same at night, after dinner, and remained there until ten o'clock when the lights were required to be out. As that hour approached, I dutifully prepared for bed but when the building grew quiet I got up and moved back to the chair, sitting there for hours gazing up at the stars. Imagining what it might be like to be at home in the chair by the window in the front bedroom on the second floor, watching Julia as she walked by with her dog.

Finally, the day arrived for my appearance in court. The deputy who had come with Fulbright to tell me of my sister's death arrived at lunchtime and drove me to the hearing in his patrol car. We parked near the courthouse entrance and he escorted me up the steps and down the hall to the courtroom where I took a seat alongside Fulbright at the counsel's table. We hadn't been there long when an attorney for the county entered and took a seat at a table to our left.

Soon after that, the judge entered. Everyone

stood while he made his way to the bench, and once he was seated we returned to our chairs. The bailiff announced our case and until then I had been calm, but as he said my name I grew tense and nervous. It sounded strange. My name. The courtroom. With the judge glaring over at me. Fulbright seemed to notice and I expected him to take my hand but instead, out of sight from the others, he rubbed the top of my thigh. At first I was taken aback by the gesture but then realized he had not wanted the judge to see lest he notice my nervousness and think it was related to my mental condition rather than to his presence.

While I struggled to maintain my composure, the attorney for the county stood and informed the court of my sister's demise. The judge already knew. Announcing it in court was merely a formality. All the same, everyone turned in my direction. I acknowledged them with an appropriate nod of my head but did not smile as might have been the custom on other occasions.

In spite of my sister's absence, the judge insisted on receiving a report from the doctor who evaluated me at Broadmoor. I assume he wanted a record of the doctor's opinion merely to protect himself should I later engage in some untoward activity. Despite my nervousness, I had every confidence that I was to be released that day. I had seen the people at Broadmoor. I was nothing like them.

Instead of accepting the doctor's report on paper, the judge called him to the witness stand and asked him to give an oral report as well. The doctor—an older man approaching retirement but still quite articulate—described his encounters with me in more or less accurate terms and summarized me as neuroatypical, a term I had never heard before but one I rather liked. Since childhood, many terms had been used to describe my personality and the manner in which I processed information, on the spectrum being the most frequent and also the one I disliked the most.

When I was eight years old, the school sent me home for being rude to a teacher. I wasn't rude. Blunt, perhaps, but not rude. Mother didn't allow us to act rudely. Officials at the school didn't agree with my assessment, however, and told Mother I should be evaluated before they would allow me to return to class. To satisfy them, Mother took me to a psychiatrist. It was my first experience with one, though by no means my last.

The psychiatrist—Dr. Malik, a crotchety man about the age of the doctor who evaluated me at Broadmoor, but with untrimmed nose hair that often was cluttered with residue of obvious origin—subjected me to a number of interviews. Interrogations, actually. Then administered a battery of tests, some of which I enjoyed very much and continued to repeat after Malik's assistants told me to stop. They tried to force me to quit but I resisted until they sent for Mother. She gave me a sip of Coca-Cola which slowed me just a little, then guided me to the window where I took another drink while I stared out on the traffic below. That was how she did it at home, too.

A few days after the final test, Mother and I went back for a consultation with Malik. The results of their work, he told us, indicated that I was brilliant in many areas, a fact that seemed to please Mother very much. "But," he added. "Your son showed considerable deficits in social skills. He also appeared unusually sensitive to light and sound."

"What does that mean?" she asked.

"It means that theoretical subjects are a simple matter for him but the normal auditory clutter that attends daily life poses an astronomical challenge to him. Has he always been this way?"

"No. When he is home he spends most of his day in his room."

"Room." Malik had a knowing tone and an accusative look in his eye. "Or closet?"

"He refers to the closet as his clubhouse."

"And friends?"

"Most boys don't have many, do they?"

"Most boys swim in a sea of testosterone," Malik replied.

Mother looked displeased. "You mentioned a social aspect."

"For one thing," Malik said, "he tends to be quite…blunt."

"Plainspoken," Mother corrected.

"No, ma'am." Malik shook his head. "Blunt. And while we were testing him, he had trouble keeping his shirt on. I think that was one of the things the school encountered as well."

"He does best when his clothes don't touch his skin."

"Yes, well." Malik defaulted to an arrogant disposition when he felt challenged. "That is rather unavoidable in some circumstances."

"That's all you found? He's brilliant but doesn't care for clothes? We already knew that."

"I'm trying to be kind," he said. I was sitting in the room while they talked and he glanced in my direction with that comment.

Mother seemed taken aback. "Why do we need your sympathy?"

"Because." Malik lowered his voice. "Based on the tests, interviews, and observations, I'm afraid I must tell you that your son is au—"

"No," Mother snapped, cutting him off. "You will not use that word over my son."

"Then what word should I use?"

"Brilliant will do just fine."

"Genius?" he said snidely.

"I'm the one paying your bill," she snarled. They appeared to have some sort of history between them but I knew better than to ask about it.

"Then let's just say, he's on the spectrum."

On the spectrum. I had no idea what that meant and on the way home I asked Mother. She smiled at me with the kindest expression of motherly love she'd ever shown. "It means, 'too brilliant for that damn doctor to handle,'" she said.

After that, I received my schooling at home through private tutors. Father arranged for it. Until I reached the ninth grade, they taught me from the comfort of my room and submitted reports of my grades to the school board. Father had friends there.

When I reached ninth grade there was a change in the school board. I was once again sent to school with the other students. It was a bit of a shock to my senses—the noise and light and the need for clothes that brushed against my skin—but I managed. And in the years that followed I heard many words used to describe me, but none of them proved adequate. And none of them as acceptable to me as neuroatypical.

That day in court, when we were there for the hearing in my case, I listened while the judge engaged the doctor from Broadmoor in a lengthy and elaborate conversation. At first he seemed really quite lost in the terms and distinctions, but slowly, incrementally, he came to an understanding of what the doctor meant by his description of me. "So," the judge said by way of summary, "he thinks differently from most people but he's not a threat to himself or anyone else." It was the closest thing to a compliment I had received from a stranger in a long time.

"That is correct," the doctor confirmed.

"Very well," the judge said. "I've heard enough."

Julia was present in the witness room that day. I caught a glimpse of her in the hallway as we arrived but Fulbright steered me away from her. She was wearing a red top with a black pencil skirt and high heels that accentuated her legs.

The man who walked with the girl through the woods behind the house was there, too. At least, Fulbright said he was that person. I wasn't certain he was the one I saw. The man at the courthouse that day was older and heavier than I remembered. Fulbright met with him while we waited for the proceedings to begin and when he returned he smelled of cigar smoke. I did not remember the man I saw ever smoking.

They were both present that day but neither of them was called to testify. After hearing from the doctor, the judge ordered me released and dismissed the petition that had been filed against me. The county attorney did not object.

When we were finished with the hearing in court and the judge released us to leave, Fulbright drove me back to Broadmoor to gather my belongings. Loading all of that into his car took longer than I expected—not even Homer offered to help—and processing me from their custody required a visit to the administration office, followed by a phone call to the judge's office, but an hour later we were on our way home. I sat in the passenger seat of Fulbright's car and stared out the window, watching as the landscape moved past. It reminded me of sitting at the window upstairs in the front bedroom of my house, only the images were brighter and everything went by much faster.

After weeks spent imagining the moment when I would finally be free again, the reality of it proved less exhilarating than I expected. The grass, it turned out, was as green from the window in the day room as it now was from the window of Fulbright's car. And the trees along the highway were the same as those on the lawn at Broadmoor. Still, I was glad to be rid of the place. Unlike the sounds from the neighborhood where my home was located, Broadmoor offered merely noise with no great purpose behind it. A cacophony devoid of rhythm, meter, or tempo save for the rise of the din in the morning and the waning of it in the evening. I found it very disorienting—even at night when the halls grew quiet and I could hear the sound of my breath again.

The trip from Broadmoor didn't take very long and soon Fulbright turned the car onto the driveway at my house. I glanced up at the windows on the second floor and they peered down at me like old friends welcoming me after a long absence. I smiled at them in return as we came alongside the house, then turned onto the concrete parking pad near the back door.

Father had the pad constructed when I was ten for the purpose of teaching me how to play basketball.

I shot baskets with him for a while on two or three occasions, but each time we were out there I became distracted after only a few minutes—usually by my reflection in the window. I made a few attempts at the basket, halfhearted at best, then spent the remainder of the daylight hours standing before a downstairs window, noting the effect my position had on the shape formed in the glass, leaning this way and that and slowly moving across the plane of its reflective surface. Father, frustrated by my lack of attention to the matter at hand, gave up and went inside. After one or two sessions of that, Father stopped insisting we play and began parking the car there when he came home in the afternoon.

That day when we arrived from Broadmoor, Fulbright and I used the key from my keyring to open the back door. As I entered the mudroom, I expected to encounter the odor of my deceased sister still lingering in the air. To my surprise it was not, but scent from the cleaning agents used by the remediation company to scour the attic was strong. A sharp, chemical odor, in fact, and after only a moment my nose began to burn.

Fulbright accompanied me as I made my way into the kitchen, then walked through the downstairs rooms, raising the windows as we went. He seemed not to notice the smell and if he did, he was unaffected by it.

When we reached the hallway by the staircase I asked, "Were you able to secure my sister's residence?"

"Yes," he said. "And from what I could see, no one had been there in several days. Perhaps longer."

"You have a key?"

"Yes," he said, then he took a keyring from his pocket and handed it to me.

We climbed the steps to the second floor—I led the way—and continued through each of the rooms, raising the windows to air out the house. Fulbright stayed right with me. I think he wanted to make certain no one was lurking in one of the rooms. Or perhaps he wanted to judge my reaction to being back there and to being in the house where my sister had died. He didn't know the history of the place. Death was nothing new to it. Or to me. I didn't care that she had died there—my sister was the third person to die in the house during my lifetime. That sort of thing meant little to me and, in fact, served to deepen the experience of residing there rather than diminish it. I was at home where I belonged among the past and its memories, and I was glad to be there.

After we'd raised all the windows on the second

floor and had gone through all of the house except the attic, Fulbright decided it was time for him to leave. I escorted him downstairs to the back door and waited while he made his way to the car, then watched from the front window to see that he really was gone. You can never be too sure about things like that. Sometimes people say they're leaving, then come back for one more thing they've forgotten they needed, or double back to look through the window and see what you're doing when you think you're alone. That's how my sister did me. Mother, too, sometimes.

In spite of my best effort to air out the house, the scent from the cleaning agents remained in the air so as Fulbright's car disappeared up the street, I moved away from the window, walked to the kitchen, and found a month-old package of bacon in the refrigerator. I switched on the radio that was tuned to the public radio station and the sound of an interviewer's voice filled the void in my mind. I listened to it while I fried the bacon.

Before long, the smell of rank bacon frying on the stove hung heavy throughout the whole house and succeeded in hiding the odor of the cleaning agents. When the strips of meat were thoroughly cooked and the fatty parts dry and crunchy, I poured the meat and grease onto a plate and set it outside by the back steps for an animal to eat. I left the greasy pan on the stove, however, which allowed the scent to waft into the air a while longer. Mother showed me that technique, though she preferred to use herbs and teas steeped in a pot of water that she allowed to slowly reduce until it scorched the bottom of the pan. "Bacon," she said, "is a measure of last resort." She wouldn't eat bacon for any reason. The animals that came to our back steps didn't have that problem, though. The meat and grease I'd set outside was gone in short order.

As darkness approached I went upstairs to the front bedroom on the second floor and sat in the chair by the window to look out over the neighborhood, as was my custom. One by one, lights came on in the houses up and down the street. A breeze came up from the south and nighttime slowly settled in place. My eyes were on the houses and the cars that passed my vantage point, then receded from view as the light melted away. All the while, though, my mind was on my sister and her demise. Not in a nostalgic manner—I wasn't lonely at all and we hadn't seen each other on a daily basis since she graduated from high school. The thing that occupied my thoughts about her was deeper than that and went to the heart of who we'd been, who we were, who I was. The thing that kept rolling around in my mind was the question of why she did it. Why did she kill herself and what did it mean?

No one in our family was particularly religious. Some would say, and some did say, that we were not religious at all. Once when we were at church, Mother declined to take Communion. Because she didn't go up, I refused to, also. That meant everyone seated on our pew had to move around us and that meant the entire church noticed—even though they were supposed to pay us no mind.

The following week, Mrs. LaRue, who taught my Sunday school class, let me know how deeply she disapproved of our action. When I suggested it revealed a serious view of the solemnity of the rite—a comment I might have delivered in a sarcastic tone—she became angry, recited her family's long history of providing priests to the denomination, and questioned the depth of our family's commitment to anything at all. I told her I didn't think we needed much of a commitment to the denomination, which she liked even less than our decision not to take Communion.

When I recounted all of that to Mother, she said it was alright if they didn't think we were religious. "Jesus wasn't religious, either." She said that often in response to many situations. Her friends—the ones who came to the house to play bridge and drink Chivas Regal all afternoon—laughed every time, but the people who attended the church where we sometimes went did not, Mrs. LaRue chief among them. They thought comments like that were sacrilegious. Mother thought their response merely confirmed that her observation hit too close to home for their comfort.

But, as I said, we were not particularly religious. Some of our Catholic acquaintances viewed suicide as a mortal sin. A sin that cuts one off from God entirely, unless it is followed by repentance and an act of contrition. Being dead, however, the one who commits suicide has no possibility of repentance and, presumably, is lost for eternity. We didn't believe that. I'm not sure what we believed, but we didn't believe that. Mother said Jesus didn't believe it, either.

Our lack of formal religious observance notwithstanding, Mother viewed self-inflicted death as a tragedy. Father saw it as a supreme act of cowardice. I saw it as the desperate act of someone who could find no other means of escaping whatever forces seized their mind.

None of us showed the slightest inclination in that direction. Even upon reflection that evening I could not fathom the notion that my sister did, either. But if that was not what happened to her, then what did? Try as I might, however, I could find no answer.

Sometime after midnight I remembered that my sister kept a diary. When she was living at home she wrote in it every night and hid it in a shoe box that was tucked in the back of her closet. I found it and read it every week. I suppose she realized what I was doing because when I looked for it later it had been moved and I found it beneath the mattress of her bed—she was that obvious about everything, though she thought she was being clever. After a while, it disappeared from beneath the mattress and I found it behind the grate that covered the heating duct in her room. Plaster dust had fallen on the floor when she removed the grate to hide it and she had not bothered to sweep it up. I was amazed she knew how to unfasten the grate but not surprised at all that she failed to notice the mess she'd created in doing so. Sometime later I checked for the diary in the duct and discovered it had been moved yet again. I never found it after that, though I suspected she placed it in the attic, but I did not care to go up there. The last time I read any of it she was beginning her senior year in high school.

Although my familiarity with my sister's diary

practices ended when she left home after high school graduation, I was rather confident she had continued the habit in one form or another. She was that kind of person—an external processor who disliked conversation. Keeping a diary was her means of unburdening her soul, though from what I read when we were younger her burdens seemed quite light.

If my sister kept a diary up to the last days of her life, it might offer clues to why she did what she did—if, in fact, she had done what they said she had done. Finding her most recent one would be a challenge but she was so obvious in everything else, I was confident that if it was in her house it would be in one of her familiar hiding places—the closet, beneath the mattress, behind the grate that covered the opening to the duct in her bedroom.

Searching my sister's house, though, would have to wait until after the sun was up. I had the key that Fulbright gave me and I was my sister's sole heir-at-law. Getting inside her house would be no problem and I had every right to be there. But entering her house right then—in the middle of the night—would attract attention from her neighbors. Which undoubtedly would involve the police. Given my recent proceedings in court, I thought it best not to attract attention of any kind to myself right then.

Finding the diary would have to wait a few hours.

While I waited, I continued to think and it occurred to me that she might have brought those diaries to my house. Or left them here when she moved on. I doubted either was true and certainly there would have been no reason for her to bring her diary with her on the day she came to kill herself—if that's how her life ended, about which I continued to harbor doubt, despite the medical examiner's opinion. Still, she might have brought them with her. My sister was fully capable of almost anything, a proclivity she had proven to be true many times. And if she did bring them here or keep them here, they almost certainly would be in one of the places she visited while she was living here—she was so unimaginative in that way. I might find them right now, right here, if I searched for them in the usual places. I might. It was a possibility. And besides, looking for them would give me something to do while I waited for the sun to come up over the trees.

From the chair by the window in the front bedroom I walked down the hall to my sister's room and searched inside the closet. Some of her clothes were hanging there—new ones, current ones, not clothing from her childhood—which told me she had been living there at least part of the time while I was at

Broadmoor. But there was no indication Gemma had been there. That was curious to me because I was confident they had been romantically involved with each other right up to the end, though I had not seen either of them since the day the court took custody of me.

At least, I didn't think I had.

One day when Homer pushed me to my room and I sat in my chair by the window gazing out at the lawn, I became aware of a scent in the air that smelled like Charlie, a perfume my sister used to wear. It was popular back then among her friends. When they were at the house and the scent was particularly strong, Father and I used to sit outside until they were gone.

Once or twice he threatened to light up a Cuban cigar he'd brought back from the Cayman Islands where he'd been to meet with one of his advisors. He was as obvious about that sort of thing as my sister—going to the Caymans to talk to a financial advisor about an account created to avoid paying US taxes. His attorney tried to tell him he should meet his offshore advisors somewhere else—Rome or London or the Bahamas, even—but he didn't listen. He did, however, bring back Cuban cigars, which his lawyer was all too glad to accept when Father gave him a few.

At the time, Cuban cigars were illegal in the United States but they were readily available throughout the Caribbean. Father always purchased a dozen or so when he was down there and brought them back in his luggage. Customs officials never made an issue of them as long as he didn't bring back too many at once, like the time he tried to bring back three boxes only to have them seized at the airport.

Mother told us we should accept the heavy perfume scent as a gift and allow it to cleanse the house of the odors we created by living there. "A chance to change the air," she would say. But after my sister and her friends had been there a while, and the scent of perfume made Mother's head ache, and Father became impatient with sitting outside, she brewed a pot of her tea and herb concoction. "Better my herb than his," she used to say. An oblique reference to his Cuban cigars.

A check of the closet in my sister's room yielded nothing. Neither did the space beneath the mattress. I looked beneath the bed, too, just for good measure, but it was empty and void—except for a coating of dust on the floor, which I noted for later reference to the housekeeper. She'd been taking liberties with her work during my absence.

The air conditioner ducts did not appear to have been disturbed recently but just to be safe I used the flashlight app on my cell phone and checked inside. I found nothing there, either.

Only the attic remained as a potential hiding place for the diaries but my sister would have had no reason to hide them up there unless that's where they'd been all along and she wanted them to be discovered when her body was found, which apparently they were not. So I decided not to go up there. The attic was hot, even at night. But more than that, the items that were stored up there held memories from the past that did not like being kept there. Especially the ones trapped inside the musty sofa and the dusty boxes behind it. Every time I went up there those memories spoke to me and the sofa and other items that had been stored there complained about the noise they made, usually in loud and angry voices that I did not like to hear. The train set in the box at the far end was nice to me. And so was the airplane that sat atop the box. They got along well with their memories and did not mind being up there alone with just the two of them for company, though they often told me how much they missed seeing me and the laughter we shared in the past. The others, though, were not as polite and after all I'd been through in the past few weeks at Broadmoor and then in court, I didn't care to hear from them just yet.

When the search of my sister's room provided nothing except the assurance that she had been living there at least part of the time while I was confined at Broadmoor, and that the housekeeper needed to pay greater attention to her cleaning tasks, I turned out the light and walked back to the front bedroom. My chair still was by the window so I took a seat on it, crossed my legs as was my customary posture, and, with my elbows resting against my thighs, sat hunched forward slightly while I once again peered out at the night view of the neighborhood.

As the hours ticked past I replayed in my mind the events of the past year. The pickup truck in Gemma's driveway, talking to Mrs. Washington by the mailbox, my sister's car replacing the pickup truck, Tony coming home early and catching them in the act. Then the trouble for me that followed. Again and again I replayed the sequence in my mind until finally it came to me. The pickup on the driveway was where the whole thing started. Until then, it had been just Gemma and Tony living next door with Gemma coming over in the morning for coffee, making obvious her desire for something more from me and, not getting it, returning home before lunch. But what if I had acted differently toward her?

What if I had relented and given her the attention she desired? The attention she craved? What if our rendezvous over coffee had become instead a rendezvous upstairs in my bed? Would I have avoided everything that followed my rejection of her? Would Gemma still be married to Tony? Would my sister still be alive? Would I have avoided Broadmoor?

Or were the seeds of the things that happened—Gemma and Tony, Gemma and my sister, Gemma and the divorce, Broadmoor—was that already planted in the soil of what had happened in the years before? Was this moment the result of events set in motion at my birth? Before my birth? Before my parents even met?

For the next several hours I stared out the window and reconstructed in my mind the events that sprang from my birth. Very quickly—much quicker than I thought possible—I strung together a series of events that led from my delivery to the time my sister graduated from high school. However, none of those events included Gemma and for a moment I wondered how my sister came to be associated with Gemma—it seemed as though her car had appeared next door without provocation or antecedent—and then I remembered they'd been friends for a long time, but not in a way that led to anything else. Theirs was a friendship that arose over horses, which is where it faded, too.

When we were younger, my sister read a novel about horses—National Velvet or Black Beauty or something like that—and developed an insatiable desire to own a horse. At first Father resisted but finally gave in and found a stable near Round Rock that boarded them. He bought a horse for her and she kept it up there. Gemma had a horse there also and the two of them used to go riding together. Mother drove her to Round Rock on riding days, usually on Saturdays but sometimes on Sunday afternoons, too. I accompanied Mother once or twice. The drive up there was pleasant and I enjoyed the hum of the tires against the pavement. The sound of it eased my mind much the same as the voices on public radio now when I play it in the kitchen.

Horseback riding lasted about a year and as Gemma and my sister grew older, their lives took them in different directions but they never quite lost touch. Then, after Gemma married Tony and moved into the house next door, they saw each other slightly more frequently but solely on a social basis. That explained their acquaintance but it didn't explain for me how my sister came to be romantically involved with her. Or how the sequence of events that caused trouble for me—first the man in the pickup truck, then my sister, then my sister running naked from the house—came to be set in motion. To get answers to those questions I needed to locate my sister's most recent diary—if one existed. Barring that, I needed to locate Gemma. She could tell me what happened. If she would.

According to Fulbright, no one had seen Gemma since about the time my sister died. Perhaps she had engaged in some nefarious or explicit act that directly caused my sister's demise and fled to avoid the scrutiny of the detective's questions. More likely, though, she had grown bored with my sister, tossed her aside in exchange for a new romantic connection—just as she had replaced the man in the pickup truck with my sister—and become distracted by the bliss of that new paramour, which would have been very much like the Gemma I knew.

Regardless of what she'd done with herself, I wanted to know what had occurred to drive my sister to her death and Gemma was the one who could tell me. So I decided to go to my sister's house as soon as it was morning and search for the diaries, then find Gemma.

When the sun appeared through the trees behind Mrs. Washington's house, I rose from my place on the chair by the window in the front bedroom and went downstairs for a breakfast of Cheerios, toast, and coffee. Milk in the refrigerator was almost sour but I used it for the cereal anyway, though not in the coffee. Mother often said, "Sour milk is okay to cook with but you can't put it in hot coffee. It'll curdle with the first drop and ruin the whole cup." That morning, I drank the coffee black, though I added extra sugar.

About eight, I went out to the garage, raised the garage door, and got in the front seat of the car behind the steering wheel. The interior of the car smelled musty and there was a thin film of mildew on the steering wheel that rubbed off on my hand when I touched it. I found a wipe in the console and wiped away as much as I could, then placed the key in the ignition and turned it. The engine turned over once, then twice, then caught on the third try and sputtered to life. I allowed it to idle a while, just to be sure everything worked. Father taught me that. "Let it run a few minutes in the morning," he said. "To get the oil circulating through all the moving parts."

When the temperature gauge moved up from the bottom mark on the dial and the oil pressure light did not come on, I was satisfied everything functioned properly. I closed the driver's door, put the car in reverse, and backed it slowly from its place in the garage. It rolled out with no problems at all and I brought it to a stop directly opposite the post for the basketball hoop. The post still was standing by the parking pad, though it was rusted from exposure to the weather and the paint on the backboard was faded.

When the car came to a stop, I reached overhead to the sun visor and pressed the button on the remote control device that activated the garage door, then watched as it slowly lowered into place. The kids who lived up the street from me used to get in there and plunder through my tools when I left it open so I waited until the door was all the way down before continuing. As it banged into place, I removed my foot from the brake and backed the car to the street, then started on my way.

My sister lived on the opposite side of town, as far away from me as she could get and still remain a resident of the same city. That's what she told me. I'm not sure I ever believed that was how she really felt, but that's what she said. Word for word. I'm not making it up. Mother did not allow us to tell falsehoods.

The house, a two-story red brick federal with white trim, sat on a large lot that was covered with oak trees and azalea bushes. Being federal in style, it didn't have a porch—just a basic box for the center of the structure with matching wings on either side—and it wasn't as big as my house, but I liked the way it looked from the street. It had a nice balance and the landscaping gave it an elegance that reflected my sister's one strength—she had a wonderful sense of style.

When Mother was alive I used to go over there with her. After she died, my sister didn't want me around so I stayed away except to bring her some food once when she had the flu and couldn't get out. All of her friends were either at work or away and she had been subsisting on crackers and hot tea until that ran out, then she got desperate and that's when she called me. I was the last person on her call sheet. Which was alright with me. I didn't call her, either.

Why she wanted that house was a mystery to me. An apartment would have suited her need for space much better, but then she wouldn't have had the same degree of privacy. Neighbors sharing a common wall, as they do in an apartment, would have been too close for her. She always felt she was hiding more than her share of issues and an apartment would have put her too close to other people to feel like she was keeping those issues out of sight. Though most of the things she thought she was hiding were not of a nature anyone else would have bothered to obfuscate in the least. The few dark secrets she did have did not affect those of us who had experienced her presence at a greater depth. We already knew her for who she really was, not the person she wanted people to see. She couldn't hide from us and trying to hide from everyone else only caused her grief, though she never understood that.

The drive to the opposite side of town was uneventful and when I arrived at my sister's house I steered the car down the driveway to a place near the steps by the back door. Driving was one of my least favorite things to do and, despite the fact that I was at her house, I was glad when the car came to a stop.

With the car parked behind the house, I switched off the engine, then stepped out to the pavement and made my way to the back door. I used the key I'd been given by Fulbright to let myself inside but as I grasped the door knob I noticed he had changed the locks but used an inferior brand. Based on articles I had read, the ones he purchased were among the least reliable on the market and I made a note to have them changed again as soon as possible.

A stale odor inside the house told me Fulbright was correct in his assessment that no one had lived there in quite a few days. Certainly not since the locks were changed and probably not for a while before then. There was a heaviness about the air, too, and when I located the thermostat in the hall I saw that the air conditioner had not been set to operate frequently. I adjusted it to a lower setting and a rush of cool air swept through the house as the system turned on. I preferred the air cool and dry. That way, it didn't touch my skin so much.

As I made my way through the downstairs rooms, nothing seemed out of place. No dirty dishes cluttered the kitchen counter or sink; no newspapers scattered about the den; not even an open book or magazine lying beside a chair or resting on an end table. All of which raised my suspicions immensely. My sister was not a tidy person and she didn't keep a tidy house. A month's worth of dust on everything was not uncommon, but there was none of that. Only a light coating, as if the house had been cleaned recently—not real recently but more recent than my sister would have done. Which was contrary to my earlier assessment that no one had been there in quite some time, but still I whispered, "It's just too clean, though. And far too organized."

Upstairs I found much the same. The beds were made with the spreads stretched tightly and the pillows tucked in place. No clothes lying on the floor. No shoes out of place. Towels in the bathroom were hung straight, square, and even. And in the closet the clothes were organized with one size hanging to the left and another to the right. Gemma and my sister were not the same size. And that's when I knew Gemma and my sister had been living there together. I was certain of it. Gemma was the one who made sure it was put in order, too.

My assessment seemed all but undeniable and to test the notion that they had lived there together I leaned close to the bed and sniffed the pillows. One side smelled of Charlie, the perfume my sister had preferred since high school. The other side smelled like a scent from Lacoste, which Gemma preferred. I'd noticed her wearing it many times when she came to the house for coffee.

Assured by the clothes hanging in the closet that Gemma had lived there with my sister, and by the scent on the pillows that they had shared the bed, I sniffed the spread on both sides and found it only smelled of Gemma, then I checked the upholstery on a chair in the corner and sniffed around over the furniture. All of it smelled of Gemma. "She was the one who straightened this place." I knew it in my heart. "But why?"

Whether Gemma had been romantically involved with my sister made no difference to me. And the possibility that I might come to the house and discover evidence of their time together was a matter of no concern to either of them. They already knew that I knew they were together. Still, Gemma had gone to the trouble of straightening up.

Perhaps, I reasoned, she felt at least a twinge of guilt at the thought of someone besides me seeing the house the way it really was after one of their sessions together. Someone besides me who might see the disheveled bedding and the underwear strewn across the floor and conclude that the nature of their encounters had been quite passionate and even reckless.

My mind raced ahead—Gemma had rushed there after my sister died to straighten things up before anyone else arrived to have a look. Before the police arrived. Before the detectives arrived. Before I arrived. And after putting things in order, she disappeared to avoid answering questions that might pry beneath the surface of what appeared to be merely a suicide.

"This orderliness," I said softly, "is actually a cover-up meant to hide the truth of what really happened here." But what had happened there? Aside from two women making love, or having sex, or satisfying some inexplicable lust, what had gone on?

Answers to my questions could not come from the house. They could only come from Gemma or from my sister's diaries, if they existed. And there was only one way to locate the diaries, so I began searching for them, starting with the drawers of the nightstands on either side of the bed.

A search of the nightstands yielded nothing and working methodically around the room, I checked ever drawer in every other piece of furniture, every duct opening, and the space beneath the mattress. Still, I found nothing of the diaries. Then I moved on to the other rooms.

As I was lowering the mattress into place on the bed frame in the guest room, a woman's voice spoke to me from the doorway. "You won't find it there." At the sound of it, I turned to look in the direction from which it came and saw Gemma standing in the hallway. "Where is it?" I asked, without explaining myself.

"She took it to your house so she could put it with

the others."

A frown wrinkled my forehead. "My house?"

"Yes."

Gemma entered the room and took a seat on the edge of the bed. "She didn't hate you, you know."

"She didn't like me, either," I replied.

"Maybe." She shrugged, then looked up at me. "Why are you here?"

"Did she have a will?"

"I don't know." Gemma shrugged again. "We didn't get that far."

My left eyebrow arched in a skeptical expression. "I think we both know how far things got."

"Yeah." A wisp of a smile came to her. "I guess we do."

"So what happened to her?"

"I don't know, exactly. We had a fight. She threw me out. I went to a hotel for a few days and then got an apartment."

I glanced around at the room. "Then you came back here to straighten up."

"No." She shook her head. "It was a mess when I left the last time."

That didn't fit with my understanding but her voice sounded genuine. "If you didn't do this," I said. "Who did?" I gestured to the room as I spoke.

"Did what?"

"Straightened up."

"She did," Gemma answered.

I shook my head. "Not my sister."

Gemma was insistent. "She kept it like this all the time."

"But you said it was a mess."

"Yes," she said. "It was always a mess after we were together. But she always put everything back in place."

"That's not how she used to be."

She had a knowing look. "You two never really understood each other, did you?"

I glanced away. "She didn't want me around."

"That's because you reminded her of your father."

I turned back to her sharply. "Our father?"

"He was all she ever talked about." Gemma gestured with her left hand. "That's why she kept the place so neat. She kept saying, 'What would Father think. He might walk in here any minute and see us.' At first I thought she was talking about the appearance of the room. Then I realized, she was talking about the two of us. Asking what her father would think about the way we were living."

My mind reeled at the suggestion of it. "She

thought of him as if he was alive?"

"He was alive. For her at least."

"How is that?"

She pointed. "You were her father."

"Me?"

"It all got twisted up in her mind there at the end."

That wasn't what I wanted to talk about so I changed the subject. "Did you know she used your pills to do it?"

"Yes."

"Did you know she was going to do that, before she did it?"

She had a smart-ass smile. "I refilled the prescription so she could have them."

"Why?"

"It was what she wanted. I loved her. So I helped her do the thing that would make her happy."

"You think dying made her happy?"

Gemma rose from her place on the bed. "I think it put an end to the torment in her mind. One minute she's afraid her father will find out what she's really like. The next minute she's angry with you for finding such peace and being so functional." She took a few steps toward the door, then turned to face me. "Somewhere in all of that, you became Father in her mind and every time she saw you, she saw him."

"That seems impossible. We were hardly together at all after she moved out. She must have known I wasn't him."

"I think she knew. And I think she didn't know. And that was the problem. Knowing you were you and at the same time knowing you were him. And then realizing how crazy that was and that there was no way to stop it. That became more than she could manage and finally she just wanted to escape."

The words seemed to find a place inside me and as I thought about what Gemma had said I gazed down at a rug that lay on the floor just past the foot of the bed. It was red and black and gold with patterns of squares and triangles forming a background that was overlaid with the shape of a panther lying at rest on its side—a female panther from the look of it.

When I glanced up from the rug, Gemma was gone, but I found her downstairs. We resumed our conversation and I asked her about the man who came to her house in the pickup truck and then he was gone and my sister's car appeared.

When she lived in the house next door to me, Gemma needed help re-doing a bathroom. That's when she thought of my sister and thought she might be able to help. Why she thought of my sister, I don't know. Gemma didn't know either. My sister never really worked at a job or acquired credentialed skills of any kind, but she had a good eye for design and a number of people were aware of it. Perhaps that's how Gemma came to think of her.

At any rate, my sister agreed to help and came to the house to have a look at the project. They talked about colors in the bathroom, then about furniture and flooring in the downstairs rooms, then marriage and relationships and how things turned out for them and how different it had been from what they'd imagined it would be when they were young. At first they talked over a cup of coffee in the nook off the kitchen but before long they were talking about those things on the sofa in the living room and then on the bed upstairs. And just like that, an affair blossomed.

Not long after things turned romantic between them, the man in the blue pickup truck—who had been hired to do the work my sister envisioned—finished the job and was gone. But my sister remained.

"Yeah. She remained." Gemma had a wistful breathiness in her voice. "We were together in that house every day until Tony came home and caught us in the shower together."

I would have been fine without that much information about my sister's life but the question about how they came to be together bothered me and I asked and that's what Gemma said. So I was stuck with the mental images. But the part she said earlier—about me replacing Father in my sister's mind—that part still bothered me.

After a while I noticed Gemma was no longer in the room and my legs were tired from standing all morning so I took a seat in a chair by the window in the breakfast room and stared out at the lawn while I thought about my sister and how she could have confused me with Father.

"It was twisted," Gemma said from behind me. Once again I was startled by her voice and by her appearance in the room. "But that's the way she talked," Gemma continued. "Especially after you went to Broadmoor."

"After I was sent to Broadmoor." I felt the need to defend myself. Someone sent me to Broadmoor. I didn't go there on my own.

"She kept a diary of all that happened between us," Gemma continued. "I think it covers most of the past five or six years."

"Five or six years?"

"Yes," Gemma replied. "That's when this started."

A sense of confusion came over me and I didn't

like the way all of this was going. Fulbright found the man who walked with the girl through the woods, but when I saw him in court he was old. He remembered walking in the woods but he said that was from years before. Now Gemma said her relationship with my sister started five or six years ago. I remembered it happening just last month.

Gemma kept talking. "I would find her at night wandering around the house, clutching that diary in her hand and saying, 'I have to hide this diary with the others. If Father finds it, he'll disown me.' When I reminded her that her father died a long time ago, she looked at me with the wildest eyes and said, 'Not him. The other one.' And once when I pressed her she took her wallet from her purse and showed me a picture in it of you. She jabbed it with her finger and said, 'That one. He will disown me.'"

"And that's why she filed the petition."

Gemma looked bewildered. "What petition?"

"The petition that sent me to Broadmoor."

Gemma shook her head. "You went to Broadmoor on your own."

"She told you that?"

"I was with her when you made her take you," Gemma explained. "We drove you out there to Broadmoor together. She tried to talk you out of it, but you insisted."

"That makes no sense," I sighed.

"None of it makes any sense."

It seemed that Gemma continued to talk a while longer but the things she'd said were overwhelming and confusing and I closed my eyes to think a moment and let them settle into the blank spaces of my mind. Slowly, imperceptibly at first, the confusion subsided, leaving only tension in its place. The tension of knowing but not knowing. Of time as a discontinuous jumble. First this. Then that. And the struggle of fitting it all in proper sequence. Had it been that long? Or was I merely…

Just then, I felt a hand touch my shoulder lightly and I opened my eyes to see the view from the chair by the window in the corner of my room at Broadmoor. Homer was standing beside me, his hand resting lightly on my shoulder.

"Mr. Dornblat." His voice was even and polite. "It's time for dinner."

At first I was confused but as I glanced around, the reality of the moment sank in on me with crushing devastation. The chair. The window. The lawn. I was in my room at Broadmoor.

Homer moved a portable table over to where I was seated, lowered it to a comfortable height, and set the meal tray on it. Chopped steak, mashed potatoes, green beans, and a roll. There was a bowl of congealed fruit for dessert and a glass of water with no ice, which was the way I preferred it. He tucked the corner of a napkin inside the collar of my shirt and stepped back, as if waiting to see what I would do.

At first I stared down at the table, wondering if I should eat. And if I should, when should I begin. After a moment, though, I lifted my head and my gaze fell on the nightstand by my bed. And I saw the paper cup for The Pill. And it was empty.

Nora Mae

A Short Story

In the afternoon, as the day wanes toward evening and a gentle breeze comes up from the south, I often sit on my back porch and drink ginger ale while listening to the doves cooing in the trees that grow throughout the garden that surrounds my house. A lush and verdant oasis, it is my refuge, my sanctuary, my place of peace and quiet, but it was not always so.

Despite the image conveyed by its present size and shape, the garden had an inauspicious beginning as a single daylily. One that arrived at my house in a plastic pot. The plant, given to me by my sister, came from the homeplace of a distant relative where my sister had been digging plants from the yard. She brought the flower to me and I named it Hemerocallis Dussie Moore, after the relative whose property it came from. Hemerocallis is the botanical name for daylily. Dussie was a long-deceased cousin from the maternal side of my father's family.

Whether my sister had permission to dig in that yard I do not know. She didn't say and I didn't ask. Mostly because I didn't care. Nor do I care now. The plant was a wonderful specimen and I was glad to have it, even if she stole it, which I am sure she did not. I just don't know for certain because sometimes my sister does things that surprise me. Not that I mind a surprise. And not that it diminishes my opinion of her. In fact, it has quite the opposite effect.

Things come to us from unexpected places—a co-worker's snappy comeback to a casual remark, the comment of a stranger uttered while waiting to cross the street, even the slogan on a t-shirt worn by a fast food patron you've never seen before. Seeing that daylily, with its deep orange bloom and dark green leaves, was just such a moment, and it brought back memories of my childhood that, though never far from my mind, often receded in the clutter of life.

After college I took a job as a staff writer with the *San Antonio Express-News*. Two years later, I moved to Atlanta for a job at the *Atlanta Journal-Constitution*. Most of my time was spent writing for the paper but I squeezed in a few hours each night working on a novel. When it was finished, I showed the manuscript to a friend. She knew an agent in New York and sent it to her. Four weeks later, I had an offer from a publisher. That first novel led to a second and then a third, and somewhere along the way I left the newspaper to write full-time on my own.

Life in Atlanta was fun and provided opportunities that were unavailable elsewhere in the Southeast. But after ten years I grew tired of the social stratification and the traditional Southern ethos. So, I packed up my belongings and returned to Texas, the land of my father and grandfather and many generations before them. The state where I grew up.

Our grandfather—whom we called Pop Pop—was a country lawyer who practiced in Brenham, a small town an hour northwest of Houston. When my father, Briscoe, graduated from law school, he joined Pop Pop and together they worked from an office located across from the county courthouse on Alamo Street. Most of their time was spent handling real estate deals, business transactions, and estate issues—wills, trusts, and probate disputes. Late in the afternoon, they could be found at a café on Baylor Street, regaling friends with stories, some of which were true.

Being lawyers in a rural setting, Pop Pop and

Briscoe sometimes were paid by clients with eggs, butter, fresh vegetables, chickens, hogs, and occasionally a cow. Neither of them, however, showed any interest in gardening or animal husbandry, unless it involved a client and there was money to be made from it. Our mother, on the other hand, had a keen interest in all things related to plants and animals. Because of her, we had a lively herd of cows, an expansive flock of chickens, a large vegetable garden, and an even larger flower garden. And equally because of her, we learned to care for all of it. We also learned their proper biological and botanical names.

All of that came back to mind when my sister handed me the daylily and from that humble beginning, I immersed myself in gardening, adding to that single plant many others. Some of them found along the roadside or growing on a ditch bank. A few were discovered in ambiguous locations—that ill-defined zone between yard and highway—though some nearby residents seemed not to share my sense of ambiguity about the location and protested quite loudly when they saw me digging them up. Still others were rooted from cuttings that I pinched off plants while strolling through public gardens and the grounds of various institutions.

Gradually, the garden took over my entire back

yard, then I let it slowly expand over the front yard as well. By growing it in an incremental fashion, I had time to think and change and rearrange. It also allowed me to avoid the yard police—those nosy neighbors who did not share my fascination with everything botanical and desired only that all the houses on the street have neatly trimmed lawns. With my stealthy approach, they either didn't notice the sprawling azaleas, camellias, sweat peas, nasturtiums and many others—the plants creeping up over time and becoming part of the existing landscape—or they enjoyed them too much to complain. I chose to think the latter—that they were mesmerized by the beauty and wonder of my creation—and took it as a compliment.

Hiram Gwinnett, who lived behind me, noticed my back yard, too, but, unlike the yard police, his was the notice of an open admirer. He often called to me over the fence that separated our property, usually with a question about the name or identity of a plant. Over the course of those conversations, I trained him to refer to them as plants, not weeds or flowers. The difference, as I often pointed out, was one of placement and enjoyment rather than an actual botanical distinction. Most of the desirable plants that people spend good money to buy today were once weeds of great disdain. A friend, for instance, spent much of his youth chopping lantana with a hoe from the family orange groves in Florida. Hiram spent an equal amount of time and energy mulching, watering, and otherwise caring for the clumps of lantana that grew as an ornamental near the corner of his house and his garage.

When I moved to the neighborhood, Hiram was already there and had been for quite some time, though no one seemed to know much about him. He was ten or fifteen years older than I—perhaps even more than that—and when I first met him, he seemed oddly aloof. However, once my garden began to expand, he warmed to me.

From comments he made in our over-the-fence conversations, I learned that Hiram was the only child of a farmer from Waycross, Georgia. He attended pharmacy school at the University of Georgia and apprenticed to a druggist in Sylvester, then bought the business. He never said how he came to live in the house behind me. I assumed he retired. We were a long way from Georgia.

A year or two after my garden overtook the back yard, Hiram died. No one knew he was gone until the mailman mentioned that mail was piling up in the box at his house and asked if I knew where he was. I went over there and collected the mail—we did that for each other occasionally—then walked to the back of the house and stood at a window near the kitchen with my hands cupped around my face to block out the light. That's when I saw him lying on the floor. At least, the body looked like it could be his. The light was gone from his eyes and his cheeks were sunken, leaving it to seem as if the carcass had been vacated from the inside and only the outline of a person remained.

A milk carton lay nearby and an empty glass was sitting on the counter. The refrigerator door was open and the light inside it still was on. And that's when I smelled the odor seeping through the windowpane and knew his body already was rank. I used my cell phone to call the police and took a seat on a lawn chair to wait until they arrived. Hiram had been a good over-the-fence friend and I preferred to remember him that way, rather than opening the door and confusing those memories with the putrid odor of rotten flesh. There was nothing I or anyone else could do for him then anyway.

Response time for a call about a dead body was a little faster than for other things, but it still took thirty minutes for a patrolman to arrive. I waited until he took my statement, then made my way back home.

A neighbor from across the street was there and she said she knew how to reach one of Hiram's relatives, so I left her to see to the details. There was no reason for me to hang around and as I walked back home, I assumed that would be the end of the matter.

However, two weeks after I found his body, there was a knock at my front door and when I went to check I saw a man standing on the porch. He was dressed in a dark gray suit with a white shirt and muted tie. His hair was short and trimmed neatly around his ears and off his collar. He seemed not to pose a threat, so I opened the door and he identified himself as a lawyer.

"Our firm represents the estate of your neighbor, Hiram Gwinnett," he said. "You are his sole heir."

After the lawyer explained everything to me, and after I decided to accept Hiram's bequest, we still had to publish notices in the newspaper and gain approval from the probate court. We sent notices of the legal proceedings to every person the researchers thought might be related to Hiram and waited the appropriate length of time for them to respond, but only the lawyer and I appeared for the court hearings.

So, once all of that was finished and finalized, I became the owner of everything in the world Hiram

Gwinnett owned on the day the milk carton slipped from his hand and he fell to the kitchen floor. House, pickup truck, financial assets. Even a second house at Apalachicola that I never knew he owned. All of it was mine, and I was overwhelmed.

At first, I didn't want to touch anything. I had seen him lying on the floor and I didn't really want to go inside the house after all of that. And even though his money and investments were in accounts that bore my name, they still seemed like someone else's property. But Nora Mae Gilbert, my next-door neighbor, insisted I had to check on things. "At least see about the house," she said. "You have to check on it. What if a toilet is overflowing? It might ruin the whole place and cost you thousands of dollars in water bills." So, after being upbraided by Nora Mae for a week or two, I finally walked over to Hiram's house.

Despite our many conversations, I had been inside Hiram's house only once before, when he called me over to look at a Camellia sinensis he was attempting to grow. He'd purchased it at one of the home improvement stores thinking he was getting a Camellia japonica. I told him to avoid those stores when shopping for plants, but he sometimes ignored my advice and what he got that day was not what he wanted. Japonica—the plant he wanted—is grown for its flowers. Sinensis—the plant he bought—is similar but grown for use in making tea.

"I don't care," he said. "I'll get a japonica somewhere else. I want to see what this one does now that it's here." And in one respect, he did precisely what I always told him he should do with his garden. Grow plants that fit a predetermined plan, but don't ignore the ones that show up.

After we looked at the bush that day and admired the leaves, Hiram invited me in for a glass of tea. At first I thought he was attempting a pun—look at my tea plant, have some tea—then I realized he hadn't noticed the connection. I enjoy tea, if it's brewed from real tea and not a concoction made from a mix, so I agreed to have taste of his. As things turned out, Hiram's tea was particularly good that day, so we sat at the kitchen table and drank an entire pitcher of it.

After we had our tea, we rode down to Stanton's and had a hamburger for lunch. That was one of the most enjoyable days of my life and we should have repeated it often, but we never did. The memory of that day was on my mind as I made my way to the back door and went inside the first time after Nora Mae encouraged me to do so.

Hiram's house key was on a ring with a medallion from the University of Georgia, the school from which he graduated. I took it from my pocket, placed the key in the lock, and gave it a turn. As the door opened, a rush of stale air greeted me full in the face. A cleaning crew scoured the kitchen floor and removed all traces of odor from Hiram's decomposing corpse. Still, the smell that day was very different from what it had been on the day we had tea together and I hesitated before moving inside.

A glance around the kitchen told me everything was okay in there, so I walked down the hall and checked the bathrooms to make certain none of the toilets was overflowing. I knew where the bathrooms were located. You can't drink an entire pitcher of tea in a single sitting without going to the bathroom at least once. After determining the plumbing posed no problem, I had a look in each of the other rooms, too.

Years before, I had been the executor of a cousin's estate in Tennessee, and I knew about going through things in an orderly manner and working methodically through the house to make certain nothing was overlooked. People have a way of putting important things in places that make sense while they are alive, but after they're gone and someone else takes over their affairs, locating those places isn't always obvious. Researchers from the law firm had already been through most of Hiram's belongings. That's how we knew about his investment accounts and the house in Apalachicola. Now, I needed to sort through it myself with an eye toward what to do with it.

The final bathroom that I checked was adjacent to Hiram's bedroom so as I came into the room and looked around, I thought about what it might be like to rummage through the drawers and closets. At once, the task seemed overwhelming and a bit too personal—the notion of sorting out his underwear drawer was more than a little off putting. But I was already in the room and I had to start sometime, so I avoided the dresser drawers and opened the closet door instead.

A bar ran from side to side across the closet, parallel to the door. Shirts hung on the left side. Trousers were in the middle. Suits, sport coats, and jackets were to the right. All of them laundered, pressed, cleaned, and in order. Shirts facing inward from one side. Jackets and coats facing inward from the other.

Grasping them four and five at a time, I removed the clothes from the closet and laid them on the bed, then checked the floor beneath. I found only a row of shoes arranged as neatly as the clothes, with casual shoes on the left and dress shoes on the right—I already knew his gardening shoes and clothes hung by the back door. In the corner of the closet to the right I found a double-barreled shotgun that I propped against the foot of the bed. A pole with a Georgia state flag attached stood in the corner to the left.

After making certain there was nothing else in the lower portion of the closet, I moved to the shelf above the bar. On the left side of the shelf was a cardboard box. I took it down and glanced inside to find it was filled with photographs. A cursory check of those on top confirmed what I already knew—none of the photos meant anything to me. And that was the difference between what I had done on behalf of my cousin's estate in Tennessee and what I needed to do for Hiram. I knew my cousin. I was one of her people. Faces in the photographs she owned were familiar to me. The names mentioned in her letters and documents were people I knew. Going through Hiram's belongings, none of it meant anything except as the remains of a friend's life.

After checking the box to make sure nothing important was hiding at the bottom, I set it on the floor and turned back to the closet. Next to where the box had been was a camera—the kind that took film—but a check of it showed there was no film inside.

Beside the camera was a thick binder with a leather cover. I took it down and leafed through the pages to find it was a wedding album with pictures of a very young Hiram standing next to an equally young woman who was very obviously the bride. She seemed vaguely familiar but I could not recall ever knowing anyone who lived in Georgia, other than Hiram.

Behind the last photo of the album was a marriage license and I glanced over it quickly to find that Hiram Gwinnett married Judy Lingo on June 17, 1964, at the Episcopal Church in Vidalia, Georgia. "Hiram was married," I whispered. "And I never knew it."

After working through Hiram's bedroom like that—going through the closet, his dresser drawers even though I didn't want to, and the nightstand beside his bed—I moved on to the next room down the hall. On the shelf in the closet was another box of photographs and beside it was a box of papers. Funeral home bills. Hospital bills. Doctor bills. At first I thought they were for Hiram's wife—which would have explained why I never knew about her—but when I checked the names, they all were for different people.

Beneath the shelf, two winter coats hung on the bar and on the floor beneath them was a box with an electric train set inside. From the age of the engine and rail cars, it appeared to be a toy from Hiram's childhood. Other than those few items, there was nothing else of much importance in the closet or the room

Earlier, as I approached the house, I was ill at ease about going through Hiram's belongings and aggravated at Nora Mae for pushing me to do it—and aggravated at myself for allowing her to coerce me into doing it. Once inside, though, the tension lifted—until I thought of opening the dresser drawers. Concentrating on the closet got me past the anxiety of the moment and made it easier to look through the room's contents. But when I entered the second bedroom, the sense of unease returned and standing there, facing the closet with only the photographs, receipts, and toy train, I was confronted by an overwhelming sense of emptiness. Almost despair.

Not the uneasiness of looking through the belongings of another. I was beyond the awkwardness of plundering Hiram's possessions. This was a profound sense of hollowness welling up from deep inside me. An emptiness at the thought that this was all that remained. An emptiness that asked, "Did Hiram really live, and die, and leave behind only boxes of photographs of people no one knew? Copies of bills with names that no one recognized? A childhood toy unused for decades? Is that it?"

Once when I was in an automobile dealership, I saw a display case that contained trophies won by a race car driver. From a distance, the trophies appeared interesting but as I approached the case, I saw that they were cheaply made of inferior wood and metal. Not only that, the metal was tarnished and the finish was gone from the wood in almost every place. The driver was deceased and I wondered then, as I did in Hiram's second bedroom, "Is this all there is to life? To live and die and leave behind only a few relics that mean nothing to anyone?"

As I stared at the box of receipts, those thoughts tumbled through my mind and I descended into the morass of dark emotion. More than gloom and doom. The bottomlessness of nothing. The emptiness of a void. The blackness of the abyss.

Rather than continuing through other rooms in the house, I returned the box of receipts to the closet, made my way to the back door, and stepped outside. Sunlight filtered through the canopy of trees that sprawled overhead—mostly live oaks and ash. And as I gazed across the back yard, a breeze swept over me. As the air brushed across my arms, I looked up to see the roof of my house rising above the fence that separated my property from Hiram's and I thought how nice it would be to have a gate in the fence so I could walk straight over, rather than being forced to make the block.

After a moment spent contemplating how to build a gate without losing the entire fence, my mood lightened, somewhat, and I started toward the street for the trip home by the long way around the block. Before I reached the first corner my mind had moved on to consider what I could do with the things in the house. Particularly the photographs. Someone in Hiram's family might like to have them. "I should contact someone," I said to myself. "And see if they're interested."

One of the people identified by the law firm as Hiram's cousin was Karen Richardson. According to the lawyers, she lived in Sylvester, Georgia. I located an address for her and wrote her a letter offering her the pick of the photographs and family memorabilia. Two weeks later I received a response indicating she would be glad to have them. Her sister, Linda, was interested in them, too. With another round of correspondence, arrangements were made for them to travel out from Georgia to see where Hiram lived and collect a few of his things.

Before they arrived, I sorted through the boxes of photographs one more time, just to make sure nothing of importance escaped me and then I set them on a table in the middle bedroom. I was glad for the cousins to come but I didn't want them to think they had the run of the place and could take whatever they wanted.

On the appointed day, Karen and Linda arrived at my house and we walked around the block to Hiram's. All the way I was wishing I had gone ahead and cut a hole in the fence so we could go back and forth easily, but my garden wasn't designed for that and I didn't want to merely hack a way through it.

When they said they wanted to come for a visit, I assumed they would glance through the boxes, giving the photos a cursory review, then proclaim their interest in them all, take a brief tour of the house, and leave. The cousins thought otherwise, preferring to discuss each photograph in detail, remembering the person or event depicted, then recalling other incidents and people brought to mind by their conversation. I brought a chair from the living room and sat to one side, listening.

By noon that first day, they had made their way through only the first box and seemed content to sit and talk and look. I, however, was famished and suggested we break for lunch. They were agreeable and I took them to Stanton's. While we ate, I told them about the day Hiram and I came there. They were particularly amused that we drank a pitcher of tea at the house before coming. Afterward, we returned to the house and they spent the remainder of the day looking, remembering, and talking. Always talking. I don't think that house ever had heard so many words as it did from those two.

At the end of the day, I was exhausted from listening and suggested we should take a break until morning. The cousins agreed and went off to a hotel. I went home and collapsed on the bed, fully clothed. I didn't awaken until sunlight came through the bedroom window the next morning.

After another day of looking and talking, the cousins decided they wanted all of the photographs. I was glad for them to have them and gave them two other items as well—a chair they said had been made by Hiram's great grandfather and a pitcher that had belonged to his grandmother. Later when Nora Mae heard what I had done, she thought they manipulated me into giving them those things, but even if they did, I didn't mind. He was their cousin, not mine. I had no sentimental attachment to the chair or pitcher. And being gracious is never a bad thing.

On the morning of the third day, we loaded the boxes of photographs into the trunk of Karen's car and placed the other items on the back seat. The chair was a tight fit, but we made it work.

As they prepared to leave, I remembered the box of receipts that I found in the second bedroom and I showed it to them. They looked through a few of the papers and then Karen said, "I know or knew all of these people, but I have no idea why Hiram had their receipts."

"So, some of them are still alive?"

Karen picked up the receipt for the funeral home that lay on top. "Well," she said. "This one's not. This is an invoice for Luther Adcock's funeral. He died before Hiram moved out here."

"We went to the service," Linda added.

"Half the town went."

"I liked the preacher's sermon."

"I hate that man."

"Let me move over a little," Linda said, I think only partly in jest. "Just in case lightning strikes."

"I'm not the only one."

"I know," Linda said. "But still. He is a preacher."

"Doesn't give him an exception."

There was a hint of coldness in Karen's voice

that I couldn't resist. "What about the preacher?"

A darkness came over her. "Get me started on that and we'll be out here another three days."

An awkward silence settled over the room, then Linda took a paper from the box. "This is a doctor's bill for Mitzy Preston. She lives up the street from me."

Everyone seemed to relax. "All of them are marked, 'Paid,'" I noted.

"Yes." Linda nodded. "They are."

"Do you think Hiram paid them?"

Karen spoke up. "There's no way of knowing."

"I can ask Mitzy," Linda offered, still holding the bill in her hand. "She and I are pretty good friends."

"You mean acquaintances.," Karen needled.

"No," Linda countered. "It's more than that."

"Not after that thing with the cat."

"Well," Linda conceded. "There is that… But I'm curious about these receipts. I'll ask her anyway. It might give us a chance to clear the air."

I was curious, too. "What's the thing with the cat?" I asked.

Karen grinned. "Linda ran over one of Mitzy's cats."

"That's what she says," Linda quipped. "I never knew I hit anything, and I still don't think I did."

Karen smiled. "But?"

"But I might apologize if she'll tell me about this bill."

The thing about the cats stuck in my mind. "Cats? How many does Mitzy have?"

"Lots." Karen sighed. "Mitzy has lots of cats."

"Too many cats," Linda noted.

"Her place smells like a litter box."

"She smells like a litter box."

"Maybe we should leave it at that."

"Good idea," Linda said. "But I'm still asking her about these receipts."

Karen gestured to the box. "Do you think we should take them with us?"

Something inside me bristled at the idea. People—especially the well-intentioned—have a way of taking a thing and running with it. If you let them, they'll take over your entire life. I wasn't sure if Karen and Linda were like that, but I didn't want to find out. The photos, the chair, the pitcher—that's all they could have of me. And of Hiram. But I remained curious to know what they might discover about the receipts. Better to write them about it, though. Later. After they were gone. "No," I replied. "I'll keep them here."

As they walked out to the car once more, I

remembered the wedding album and asked about Judy. They both looked at me with blank expressions. Karen finally said, "I have no idea what you're talking about."

"Me, either," Linda added. "We've never known Hiram to be married to anyone."

They waited while I retrieved the wedding album from the closet and brought it to them at the car. Neither of them said a word as they leafed through the pages until they reached the license that was tucked in back. Karen pointed to the first witness signature. "Randy Starnes was Hiram's best friend from high school."

Linda pointed to the second one. "That's Pete Whiteside. Another of his high school buddies. I saw Pete at the grocery store the other day."

"So, who is Judy Lingo?" I asked.

"Maybe she was someone he knew from college," Karen suggested. "According to this license, they got married in 1964. Hiram would have been about twenty years old."

"Twenty-two," Linda corrected.

"Yeah," Karen agreed. "So maybe that's what it was."

Linda frowned. "But then, she would have been with him when he came to Sylvester."

Karen nodded. "Maybe."

The way they talked left me wondering how they knew so many details, but I decided to let it pass. They were leaving. I was ready for them to go and didn't want to chase down one more rabbit hole of who-was-where and what-was-what.

"Well." I reached out for the album and Karen handed it to me. "When you get back to Georgia, maybe you could find out about Judy, too."

"Yes," Karen replied. "Maybe we can."

"We'll put her on the list," Linda added. "It'll be like homework."

We said goodbye once more, then they got into the car and started back to Georgia. When they were gone, I went inside the house and returned the box of receipts to its place on the shelf in the closet of the middle room, then checked to make sure the lights were off and locked the door on my way out. But I brought the wedding album with me to my house.

2

Almost every afternoon when I went out to sit on my back porch to enjoy the view of the garden, and listen to the doves cooing in the trees, Nora Mae appeared at the corner of the house, mail in hand, fresh from her walk down to the mailbox by the street. Naturally, I could not shoo her away and, having a cold bottle of ginger ale in my hand, I could not ignore the fact that she had none in hers, so I always offered her one. I kept them in a cooler on the porch. It was no difficult matter to say, "Grab a bottle from the cooler, Nora Mae." And she always did.

Sitting there on the porch together, we talked about whatever came to mind, and when she finished her ginger ale and it was time for her to go, she rose from her chair and started for the steps. But just before going down she always glanced in my direction and said, "I might be gone by morning. When they come to get my body, make sure you tell them who I am."

At first it bothered me that she talked that way—an obvious allusion to death—but after she'd said it a dozen times I realized all she wanted was to make certain someone noticed her presence. To be sure someone marked her down as in attendance that day and noted that she was yet among the living. Being the most recent addition to the neighborhood—and the youngest—I was the designated recipient of her daily entreaties, others on the street having long since written her off.

Layton, who lived on the opposite side of her, said she was crazy and refused to answer the door when she came over. Augusta, who lived across the street, stopped returning her calls long before I arrived. And Harry, who lived on the opposite side of me once shot her dog, so they had nothing to do with each other except to exchange complaints with the police.

As for me, I always enjoyed a good story. Which meant Nora Mae and I spent many hours together on the porch. Talking. Listening to her was much easier than listening to Hiram's cousins. I didn't know them. Or any of the people they mentioned.

Nora Mae grew up in Euless, a town that eventually became a suburb of Dallas. When she was a girl, it still was a long way from anywhere. Oliver Hale, Nora Mae's great grandfather on her mother's side, moved there with his family when he was ten years old. Not long after they arrived, Elisha Euless, for whom the town was named, built a cotton gin. Oliver went to work there the summer he turned twelve. He worked at the gin—and later at Euless' sawmill—until he was twenty, then he met Delia Northcutt, the woman who became Nora Mae's great grandmother.

After that, Oliver didn't want to be anywhere Delia wasn't, so he opened a blacksmith shop in a barn not far from the cotton gin and went to work for himself. With the profit from the shop he bought a house on Main Street and married Delia. Not long after that, they started producing children. As Nora Mae described it, "One child per year for the next twelve years—almost—there was a break in there between some of them—but they all survived to adulthood."

When she told me that part about all of them surviving to adulthood, I wanted to call bullshit on it. Times were tough back then. Many children did not even survive delivery. But Nora Mae showed me clippings from the newspaper to prove it. Several years earlier, a reporter from the *Euless Times Democrat* heard the story and was as skeptical as I, but he had the time to research it and he wrote an article for the paper about how it was absolutely true. I read the article.

The lives of Oliver and Delia—and, by extension, Nora Mae—might have followed a different path but one day Moses Watson brought his two-horse surrey to Oliver's shop. The surrey needed a new axle and the horses needed to be re-shoed. While Oliver did the work, Moses got into a card game and lost big. So big, he couldn't pay for the work on the surrey or the stable fees for the horses. Eventually, after several long and heated arguments, Moses surrendered the surrey and horses to satisfy the bill.

Every Sunday after that, Oliver and Delia tooled around town in that surrey with their children seated behind them. They were a sight to see and the talk of the town, with everybody asking on Monday, "Did you see the Hales on their ride yesterday?" And people reckoning the quality of their Sunday afternoon by whether they did or not.

Finally, Harold Barnett decided he wanted Oliver's surrey and horses as a present for his wife. "She wants to ride around like that on Sunday afternoon and you're the only one in town with a surrey that nice."

At first, Oliver was reluctant to trade, but Barnett kept offering more and more until finally Oliver said, "I tell you what, Harold. I'll swap you that surrey and the horses that go with it for that forty acres you own out by Denham's Creek." No sooner were the words out of Oliver's mouth than Barnett thrust his hand toward Oliver to shake on it and said, "Deal."

For six months after that, there was no Oliver and Delia riding around town on Sunday afternoons with the kids seated behind them. And there was no peace in the Hale household, either. Delia was mad.

In the seventh month, a man by the name of Quarrels came to town riding in a two-horse surrey with a leather top and fringe hanging from the edge all the way around the top. He stopped at the train station where he found a telegram waiting for him. It seemed he'd been traveling for two weeks, making his way east from Albuquerque and stopping at every station along the way to telegraph his wife in Slidell. She was pregnant and due almost any day. When he checked at the Euless station, he learned that she was in labor. "Get here quick," was all the message said.

Needing a ticket on the afternoon train, Quarrels asked around town about a loan or a deal or a handout or anything to help him on his way. "It'll take a week to get there from here by carriage and I can be there tomorrow on the train." The storekeepers and the banker were sympathetic to his situation but unwilling to advance any money. Only the Methodist minister was willing to help, but he had no means by which to do so.

The minister, however, knew the inside story on almost everyone in town and brought Quarrels to Oliver and soon a deal was struck. Forty dollars for the horses and the surrey, with Quarrels having the right to buy them back at the same price plus ten dollars if he came through town again and wanted them. "Provided," the minister added on Oliver's behalf, "the horses are still alive."

"Deal," the man said.

Money changed hands. The horses were stalled, watered, and fed in the barn at the blacksmith shop. The surrey was parked outside for a fresh wash. And Quarrels made the afternoon train headed east as fast the locomotive would go. The fireman, Oliver's first cousin, kept the firebox stoked with extra coal and they highballed it all the way.

The next Sunday after that, Oliver was once again at the reins of a two-horse surrey, this one even better than the first. Delia, looking proud and dignified, was seated next to him with their children all around, laughing and carrying on like they had good sense.

Soon after, Oliver and Delia began having children again and before long, they were riding in that surrey with twelve children seated beside them and behind them—and the extra ones hanging off the back. The youngest of those children was Hubert, Nora Mae's grandfather and the last child Oliver and Delia ever had.

Hubert grew up in Euless and eventually took Oliver's place as the town's blacksmith. By then, however, smithing wasn't as profitable as it had been, but Hubert had seen the end coming and opened the town's first automobile dealership—Hubert Hale Motors—in a building next to the barn where the blacksmith shop had been.

Hubert had hoped for a son to take his place but had three daughters instead and learned that women could do anything a man could do and sometimes do it better. The youngest was Ida, Nora Mae's mother. She was the first in the family to attend college, doing so in Austin where she met Tommy John Gilbert. Tommy John was a man of vision and ideas. "Entertainment is the thing of the future," he often said, and he envisioned a string of movie theaters reaching from Amarillo to Houston. "Even all the way to New

Orleans," he sometimes added.

No one paid much attention to Tommy John or his ideas, but Hubert thought Tommy John might be onto something. Yet even using rudimentary math and figuring with a pencil on a writing tablet at the kitchen table Hubert came to a serious obstacle. "A venture like that would require capital we don't have."

And that's when someone suggested Hubert find out more about the black slick that formed from time to time in a low spot on the forty acres that Oliver received from Harold Barnett when they traded for the original two-horse surrey a hundred years before. And that's when they found oil. Lots of oil.

Not long after that, movie theaters started showing up in towns and villages across south Texas. They attracted lots of attention, too, and with all of those people standing around waiting for the next show, Tommy John saw another opportunity. "We need to sell them something," he said. And soon after that, shopping centers sprang up next to the movie theaters. As time went by, many of those centers became malls. Some of them quite large. All of them very valuable.

Tommy John was a man of vision and insight. Hubert knew a good thing when he saw it. And Nora

Mae never lacked for money a day in her life.

When she told me that story I was quite entertained but it sounded too much like a typical Texas tale, which made it a tall tale and just another of the many fabrications that made Texans interesting. Except, in this instance, the movie theaters actually existed and so did the shopping malls. I knew where five of the original theaters were located. Nora Mae's sister, Louise, ran the company that managed them. And Hubert Hale Motors was right there on Main Street in Euless for anyone to see, along with the five others opened in Fort Worth by Nora Mae's sister, Irene.

Nora Mae talked to me about that sometimes—the trust that held the rights to the forty acres, the way the dealerships and the malls and the movie businesses were owned. About the wily nature of her sisters and how just because you have relatives doesn't mean they all know how to relate.

Even from our first conversation on the back porch, I sensed there was more to the story than just sisters who couldn't get along, but Nora Mae didn't elaborate and I didn't push the issue. Secrets come out best when they come out in their own time and I assumed hers would too, eventually. Most afternoons we just talked about the flowers in my garden or the birds in the trees or the noise from the highway we heard in the distance.

Things remained that way between us, following a comfortable rhythm. She came over in the afternoon, we sat together on the porch enjoying the garden view. But not long after Hiram's cousins returned to Georgia, I mentioned to Nora Mae that I had found a wedding album in the closet at Hiram's house. That's when the secrets began to emerge.

"Did you know Hiram had been married?" I asked the question as a conversation starter, thinking she probably had no idea whether he had or not—though she had lived on our street longer than anyone and there was always the possibility.

Nora Mae was silent a moment, then she looked over at me. "Yes," she said softly. "I knew."

My eyes opened wide. "How did you know that?"

She cleared her throat. "Because I had an affair with his wife."

Her response left me astounded and for a moment I didn't know what to say. Nora Mae noticed the look on my face and gave me a coy smile. "Rather shocking, isn't it?"

"You had an affair with Judy Lingo?"

Nora Mae nodded her head. "She and I met during freshmen orientation."

"So, how did she end up with Hiram?"

"Judy knew she was attracted to women, but she felt guilty about it. She'd struggled with it since puberty. Maybe even before. I'm not sure. But she tried to be the person everyone wanted her to be, but she just didn't care for boys that way. So, when she got to college, she decided to live the way she really felt. But after our first year, she told me she couldn't do it anymore and that's when she started seeing Hiram."

"And they got married."

"Yes," Nora Mae replied. "The next summer."

"But I'm guessing you and Judy couldn't stay away from each other."

She took a sip of ginger ale. "And you would be correct," she said.

"And Hiram found out about it?"

"Judy told him."

"He didn't know about her…situation before that?"

She seemed amused. "You find this difficult to discuss, don't you?"

"No," I said. And I really didn't. I just didn't know the correct terminology. I sipped from the bottle in my hand, then said, "You can be whomever you want to be. And you can be with whomever you choose. I just don't know the correct terms for the topic."

"Hiram knew nothing about her being lesbian," Nora Mae said.

"And how did he take it when he found out?"

"Not as well as you are."

"What happened?"

"He tried to live with it, but she didn't want to be a man's wife and she couldn't make herself enjoy it."

"So, she tried coming out, then she tried being straight. Then she gave up and just went back to being…who she really was?"

Nora Mae grinned. "I like watching you squirm."

"I'm not… Well." My shoulders slumped. "Okay," I admitted. "I'm squirming, but not because the topic offends me."

"Just makes you feel awkward," she quipped.

"Yeah." I took another sip. "Awkward."

We sat in silence a moment, then I said, "What happened to Judy?"

"She moved in with a friend of ours. A girl named Rita, from Tallahassee."

"She didn't move in with you?"

"No." There was a hint of disappointment in her voice. "We weren't together very long. I didn't even know she'd left Hiram until after they divorced."

"Is this why your sisters don't come around? Because you're lesbian?"

She waited a moment before saying, "That's a complicated story."

I smiled in her direction. "Need another ginger ale?"

"Something stronger than that," she replied.

"Wait here."

I went inside and found a bottle of Jack Daniels whiskey in the cabinet, dusted off two glasses, and added a couple of ice cubes to both, then brought them out to the porch. "There's a Coca-Cola in the cooler," I said as I returned to my seat.

She pointed to the bottle. "I take mine straight."

I poured a glass half full and handed it to her, then reached in the cooler for the Coke. As we settled into our first sip, I said, "Okay. You have something stronger. Tell me about the complications."

Nora Mae took a sip from her glass, held it on her tongue a moment, before letting it slide slowly down her throat. Finally, she said, "My daddy wanted a boy but all he and Mama got were girls. Mama died giving birth to me, so I was the youngest, which meant Daddy and I spent a lot of time together. I grew up wanting to please him. He was going through a tough time with Mama dying and all."

"Is this going to get really awkward?"

She whapped me on the arm and snapped, "Not

like that!"

"I don't mean anything against your daddy. I'm just checking to see what's coming next."

"Do you want to hear about it, or not?"

"Yes," I said. "I want to know."

Nora Mae took another sip from her glass, but didn't say anything, so I prompted her. "Your father dressed you as a boy. Then what?"

She took another sip. "He dressed me as a boy." She seemed to force the words from her mouth. "And he called me Johnny. Everyone thought it was cute."

"Was it difficult?"

"No." She seemed to relax again. "I actually found it exceedingly comfortable and even after Daddy got reconciled to Mama dying and he didn't spend so much time with me, I kept dressing like a boy."

"Even after you started to school?"

"I lived that way from the time I can remember until the summer I graduated from high school. Everyone in Euless knew me as Johnny Gilbert."

"No one harassed you over it?"

"One or two tried, but I put them in their place. Everyone else was smart enough to keep their opinions to themselves."

"And they called you Johnny."

Nora Mae nodded. "Even my sisters called me Johnny."

"So, they were supportive?"

"At first. When they were young, they thought it was funny but after they got old enough to understand things like that, they were embarrassed." She looked over at me. "I had my hair cut about like yours and I wore men's clothes."

"And they didn't like it."

She looked away. "We haven't really talked much since I graduated from high school."

Something in her voice made me suspicious. "And I'm betting there was a reason for that besides what you've told me."

A smile turned up the corners of her mouth. "My oldest sister, Lucille, had a friend."

"A boyfriend?"

"No." She shook her head. "A girlfriend. She was several years older than I was, but I thought she was the most beautiful person in the world. She seemed to think the same of me."

My eyes opened wide once more. "Oh."

"Yeah," she sighed. "That's when I learned how two women give each other…the pleasure of a physical relationship."

Her cheeks turned a darker shade of pink than

normal and I grinned. “Now who’s feeling awkward?”

Her voice took a sarcastic tone. “Despite the way they talk about sex on television, most people—gay, straight, or indifferent—don’t like talking about the intimate details of their lives.”

“And Lucille got mad about that? About the way you felt toward her friend?”

Nora Mae sighed. “Someone saw us together.”

“You and Lucille’s friend?”

“Yeah.”

“Together as in…together?”

She scowled. “We were naked in the backseat of her car. Okay?”

“And that’s how you became a lesbian?”

“No.” Her scowl changed to a look of disdain. “You think it was a choice?”

“I don’t know.”

“Did you choose to prefer women?”

“No.” I shrugged. “I don’t think so.”

“That is your preference, isn’t it? Women?”

“Yes,” I replied.

“Do you remember a time when you thought it through and decided that’s the way you would be?”

“No. It was just there.” That was the truth. I remembered that much. When I reached puberty, sexual awareness sprang up inside me. Leapt up, actually. Exploded, to be more exact. There was no time for choosing or deliberation. Almost overnight, my sense of being was oriented in every way around an inexplicable urge toward members of the opposite gender.

"Okay," she said. "That's the way it was for me. At puberty, when all the other girls were interested in boys, I was interested in girls. That thing you feel when you see an attractive woman, that's how I feel when I see them, too." She shook her head in dismay. "Choice," she scoffed. "It's not a choice. When people come of age, sexuality is on them before they know what's happening. It's just that, for some people, it appears one way and for others, another."

"So, Lucille was angry because you were with her friend, or because you were with a woman?"

"She was mad because the boys who saw us were people she knew, and they talked about it. A lot."

"And she was embarrassed."

"She was many things." Nora Mae looked over at me and held out her glass. "Give me another shot of that Jack Daniels." That's when I noticed her glass was empty and I reached for the bottle. "Two fingers," she said, indicating how much she wanted. I put a little more than that in the glass, added some to mine, then set the bottle beside my chair.

"So," I said after a moment. "Why was Hiram living here, right in your back yard?"

"He didn't know I was here when he bought the house."

"When did he find out?"

"About a year later."

I gave her a perplexed expression. "It took that long for him to find out you were his neighbor?"

"I don't go around to that side of the block, as a normal thing. And he didn't come over on this side, except once or twice when I saw him over here with you."

"What did he say when he found out you lived here?"

A smile turned up the corners of her mouth. "He just shook his head and said he'd come all the way out here to get away from everyone who ever knew him, and here I was. Someone who knew his secrets."

"Did you?"

"Did I what?"

"Did you know his secrets?"

"Not many. But I'll tell you one thing." She paused long enough to sip from her glass. "Those cousins you had over there looking at his stuff, they didn't know him, that's for sure. They knew him after he graduated from college, but they didn't know him before then. They only knew him after he came to Sylvester to run that drugstore."

"So, Hiram was okay living that close to his ex-wife's lover?"

She avoided my gaze. "Whatever happened between us happened a long time ago."

"Why didn't you say something to me about this before?"

She looked over at me once more. "My life's not an open book, you know."

"But you knew I was wrestling with what to do about Hiram's belongings."

"This isn't a part of my life I like to talk about."

We sipped and rocked in silence for a while, then I asked, "Is Judy still alive?"

Nora Mae stared ahead, her eyes focused on the garden, and took another sip. "She died."

"When?"

"A few years ago."

"How did you find out?"

"Rita called me."

"You two are still in touch?"

"Yeah."

The tone in her voice said Nora Mae was through talking about her past, so I said, "Do you think I made a mistake giving those photographs to the cousins?"

"It was alright," she replied.

"Did you want them?"

"No." She shook her head slowly. "I wouldn't have known any more about the people in those pictures than you did."

"What would you have done with them?"

"Burned them, probably."

"Why?"

"Those pictures are all from the past," she said. "Nothing good can come from dragging the past into the present."

"We've been talking about the past."

"I know."

"And I think some good has come from it."

"Maybe so. But we know each other. We don't know anything about the people in those pictures. We'd just be dredging up shit we don't understand. Pardon my language."

"Do you really think that?"

"No telling what we'd find if we started digging around in that box."

"The whole thing seems sad."

"What whole thing?"

"To live all your life, and die, and all that remains is a house full of furniture no one wants and photographs of people no one remembers."

"Life is a fleeting thing."

"If we had burned all those photographs and destroyed the remaining papers, there would be nothing left of Hiram's life."

"You think there should be more?"

"Yes."

"I don't know what good holding on to a bunch of photographs does for him."

"But who will remember who he was?"

"We would remember."

"And after we're gone?"

"Like I said, do you think it should be different?"

"I think a person spends their life looking for meaning and significance, and with great effort they noodle out a little bit of it, and then they die and everything around them dies, too. And in a generation, the memory of them is gone."

She had a knowing smile. "We still remember Mark Twain."

"But not his brother," I responded.

She raised an eyebrow. "I didn't know he had a brother."

"And that's my point," I said, gesturing with my glass.

By then, afternoon had faded into evening and

darkness was coming on. Nora Mae tipped up her glass, drained the last drops from it, and handed it to me. "This is a depressing conversation," she said.

"Maybe we should sing a song or tell a joke."

"Huh. I have things to do." She stood to leave, then paused and looked back at me. "You remember what to do?"

"Tell them who you are."

"And?" She elongated the sound of it for emphasis.

"Pull you out before you start stinking." After the way we found Hiram's body on the kitchen floor, she had added that to her goodbye litany. She didn't want her body left to rot in the house like his.

"Be a good neighbor," she said, "and don't forget." Then she pushed open the screened door, plopped down the steps, and disappeared into the night.

3

After Nora Mae went home, I sat on the porch and watched while nighttime slowly enshrouded the garden with darkness. As the evening cooled, mosquitoes appeared, but the screens on the porch kept most of them at bay. There was a ceiling fan overhead and I turned it on for good measure. The breeze it generated felt pleasant and bugs that wriggled through the screen were quickly whisked away.

As I settled into my chair once more, I poured the last of the Coca-Cola from the can into my glass and added more Jack Daniels. Then added a little more.

The conversation that afternoon was, as Nora Mae pointed out, depressing. To think that we live and die and all we leave behind are the things we collect. Bits and pieces of this and that. A generation, perhaps, to remember us. And in a hundred years, all is forgotten and gone. No trace of us or anything we did remains.

Even in my own experience, I knew the names of the people who owned my house before it became mine—Maude and Simon Barnett—but who owned it before they? And who owned it before anyone thought of adding streets and houses? What were they like? What were their hopes and dreams and how much of it did they achieve? Did they make a meaningful contribution to the human conversation? To advance us forward even a little? Did they try? I doubted anyone knew or would ever know. Not now. Not after so many years passed and so many memories were lost.

And who would know about me? Would I sink beneath the ocean of time, my entire life submerged in the expansive void of the past, leaving no trace of my presence? No hint that I ever had existed?

As I sat there on the porch, an odd sense of disconnectedness came over me and I felt myself becoming distant from myself—and from reality. As if I was, right then, sinking into the abyss. Buried alive in an anonymous grave. With no one on the surface above me to know or care that I was trapped below. No one to hear my cry for help. No one to come and find me.

No one to even think that I might exist deep down, below, far below, in the darkness of nothing.

With the glass still in my hand and those thoughts tumbling one after another through my mind, my heart rate quickened. Sweat formed on my arms and back. My shirt stuck to my wet skin. And my mind raced faster and faster.

Was this a heart attack? Was I thinking those thoughts because I had reached the end? Would my next breath be my last?

One thought cascaded onto the next and I felt as though I were trapped. First in a grave. Then in a box. And a darkened room, groping for the light switch, the door, the way out, anything to restore a sense of relevance to my mind. To see. To know. To relate.

In desperation, I stomped my foot and felt the impact of my heel against the wooden floor. The concussion of the impact vibrated up my leg and reverberated through my body and somehow jarred my mind into an instant of self-awareness. In that sliver of clarity, I spoke aloud to myself. "Calm down," I said. "Think. Just think."

Hearing the sound of my voice expanded my sense of self-awareness and I used the moment to make an inventory of my body. There was no pain in any of my extremities. None down my left arm. None in my head. And the thought came to me that I should stand up, leave the porch, and step out to the garden. I did and made my way up the path that ran through the center of the garden as far as the fence that separated my property from Hiram's.

Now and then a mosquito buzzed around my ear and I felt one or two strike my legs near the ankles, but the relief of being in the open, with the sky above me, the night air against my skin, and the flowers all around, made the annoyance of the bugs seem a small thing.

At the fence, I looked up at the sky, spread my arms wide, and took a deep breath, allowing my lungs to fully inflate. I held it there a moment, then exhaled and repeated the same process.

Slowly, the distance between me and myself shrank and I returned fully to the moment. The sound of the night became clear again. A cricket chirping. An owl warbling in the tree that stood in Nora Mae's back yard. A peacock calling for its mate—someone who lived three streets over had four of the birds that wandered the neighborhood. Listening to the chorus of nature, the panic that had seemed on the verge of overwhelming me just moments earlier faded away and my body relaxed.

With my body at ease, I lowered my arms to my side and my thoughts returned to the earlier questions of life and death and meaning. While Hiram was alive, his house, the gardening, our conversations over the fence, were things of purport. They had substance.

That sounds like I knew him well, though I did not. Or that we meant more to each other than I've made it seem—and perhaps we did. But going through his belongings had been a far deeper experience for me than I had expected. I was a stranger to his past and in sorting through the things he left behind, I realized just how lifeless they were without his presence. How gone he really was. And how gone I will be when I die.

When Hiram died, the life that infused our conversation and our interaction ended. Without him, the things he left behind appeared much the same as his corpse had seemed when I saw it through the kitchen window—a hollow, lifeless shell of what once had been. Resembling him, but not really him any longer. The essence that gave vibrancy to whatever we shared was gone and the emptiness left behind by its absence was obvious.

And that's when I realized that whatever Hiram and I experienced—whatever Nora Mae and I experienced, whatever I experienced with anyone else—the vibrancy of it was in the interaction. The mutuality. The relationship.

Our relationship, however imperfect it might have been, was the thing that brought value and meaning to the moment. Without that relationship, the objects left behind were little more than lifeless remnants. Corpses of individual occurrences. Skeletal remains. The once vibrant body having lost the meaning and purpose that gave it life.

As I mulled those thoughts around in my mind, I remembered Hiram's cousins. Photographs in the boxes meant nothing to me. They were, in effect, a collection of dry bones from a past I knew nothing about. But the cousins knew the faces and the context from which those images sprang and instantly infused them with life once again. Giving away those photographs was the best thing I could have done. Had I kept them, they would have remained lifeless and, eventually, would have been thrown out with the trash. Or burned, as Nora Mae suggested. Hiram would have been lost forever.

And it occurred to me that by leaving Hiram's house and the remaining contents untouched, I was merely preserving the sense of death that invaded it when he died. Giving away his things was the only way to reverse that.

"Give away the parts that have no meaning to me," I said. "Keep the ones that do and fold them into my own experience."

The part that meant the most to me was the garden Hiram attempted to create in his back yard. Our conversations, our interaction, our relationship was focused on that and I knew instantly what to do with it. I would combine his garden with mine.

Rather than waiting to test the thought or consult an expert on whether keeping Hiram's property was the best and wisest course of action, I returned to the house, found a notepad at my desk, and made a sketch of the two yards as they existed. Then I made another sketch of how they might be transformed into a single garden.

Designers say that a first idea is often good but it's an idea anyone could imagine. So, I set that first sketch of the combined space aside and pushed my idea to the next level. Then I pushed it to the one after that and finally, sometime after midnight, I had a plan that I liked.

When I awakened the following morning, I waddled into the kitchen, brewed a pot of coffee, and sat at the table with a cup while I reviewed the many versions of garden plans that I had created the night before. The final one still seemed the best, so I resolved to begin working on it that day.

After a second cup of coffee, I retrieved a hammer and crowbar from the tool shed and walked up the path to the fence. In only a few minutes, I had pried loose enough boards to create an opening and before long the only thing that remained of the fence were the posts that once held it in place.

By the time I gathered and stacked the boards from the fence, it was almost noon. Before returning inside for lunch, I walked over to Hiram's house and wandered through the rooms, mentally inventorying the furniture. One or two pieces seemed interesting to me and he had several lamps that were serviceable. The rest appeared rather common and I decided to ask Nora Mae if she wanted any of it.

That afternoon, when Nora appeared at my back porch, I suggested we take our ginger ale and walk over to Hiram's.

"What for?" she asked. I could tell from the look on her face that she didn't really want to go.

"I've had another look around," I replied. "And I think you should, too."

"There's nothing over there I need to see."

"Have you ever been inside the house?"

"No."

"Then how do you know there's nothing in there you'd be interested in."

"Call his cousins back if you're interested in giving it to someone who cares."

Rather than concede the point, I handed her a bottle of ginger ale, took her by the arm, and ushered her down the steps to the garden path. "Come on," I insisted. "I'll be with you every step of the way."

When we reached the back door of Hiram's house, I took a key from my keyring, inserted it into the doorknob, and gave it a twist. Just then, Nora Mae grabbed my wrist to stop me. "Does it still smell?" she asked.

"It smells like Hiram," I replied. "But not like his dead body." She relaxed her grip on my arm and I pushed open the door.

Nora Mae sniffed the air as we entered the kitchen. "You're right," she said. "It smells like Hiram." I wanted to ask her more about that but thought I should keep the focus on her and the house, rather than on the recent nature of her relationship to him and how she knew what he smelled like.

As we moved through the kitchen, she opened the cabinet doors and glanced inside. At first, I thought she was merely curious but then I realized she was searching for something. I kept quiet and let her look, curiosity doing more to calm her emotions than I ever could.

In the dining room there was a china cabinet, one of the few pieces I liked. When Nora Mae opened the doors to look inside, her face lit up. "That's his mother's china," she said.

"Hiram's mother?"

"Yes."

"You knew her?"

"Not well. They took me to eat at his parent's house twice. Before Hiram found out why Judy and I spent so much time together. Both times, his mother used this china."

"His parents lived in Waycross?"

"Yes."

"Would you like to have it?"

"The cousins didn't want it?"

"I didn't show it to them."

"They weren't close," she said. "I doubt they ever met Hiram's mother."

"You shall have it," I said. "We'll bring some boxes and carry it to your house."

She seemed pleased with that idea but reluctant to follow through. "Why me?"

"These dishes have meaning and purpose for you," I replied.

"And not to you?"

"To me, they are merely nice dishes. But with you, they have life."

She gave me a look. "You're a philosopher now?"

"Just a man, wrestling with the scars of life."

"Okay," she said, finally. "I know right where I'll put them."

From the dining room we moved down the hall and checked the bedrooms. Nora Mae shared my opinion of the furniture. "Pedestrian," she said. "Although the lamps might be useful."

"Do you want them?"

"No." She shook her head. "What are you going to do with this house?"

"Use it as a guesthouse, I think."

"Then the lamps might find a place here," she noted. "Are you sure you don't want to keep the furniture?"

I shook my head. "It has no meaning for me. And I don't care for the style."

"And with the money he left," she suggested, "you can buy whatever you want."

"Exactly."

There seemed nothing more to address and I was thinking the afternoon was about to end, until we came to the living room. As we entered the room, she put her hand to her mouth, and I noticed her eyes were full. I followed the focus of her gaze and saw that her eyes were fixed on an end table. It was made of dark wood—aged mahogany or oak, perhaps—with a leather top. The leather had been polished and worn and used and had a beautiful luster. It was one of the few pieces I admired.

"You recognize the table?" I asked, knowing full well that she did.

Nora Mae nodded her head. "Judy bought it at Cardwell's Furniture Store in Augusta not long after they married. I helped her pick it out."

"Then we will carry it to your house right now."

Tears trickled down her face as she looked over at me. "You don't mind?"

"Not at all. I want you to have it. It's yours."

"But you've already given me the china."

"Do you want the china cabinet to put it in?" I asked.

"No," she answered. "I have a place for the dishes but not for a china cabinet."

"Then come on." I picked up the end table and started toward the door. "Let's take this over to your house and find some boxes for the dishes."

Packing the dishes took an hour or so and then Nora Mae brought her car around and we loaded the boxes in the trunk, rather than making multiple trips lugging them to her house on foot.

Later that week, a recycling center came for the mattresses and boxed springs that were on the beds. The Salvation Army took the furniture. Only the lamps, china cabinet, and kitchen table remained. I decided at the last minute to keep the table. It meant something to me.

With the house emptied of its contents, I turned my attention to the yard. A teenager who lived at the end of our block came to help me and we removed the fence posts. Then we went to work deconstructing and reconstructing what had been Hiram's back yard. Redefining the space from his to mine. Giving it a new sense of life. Transforming it from Hiram's yard to my garden.

Most of Hiram's property was covered in shade. Grass grew only in two small patches near the garage. The rest of the area behind the house was bare dirt, which he always raked clean and swept smooth. Because it couldn't grow a lawn, he made sure not a single sprig of grass crept in. The ornamentals he grew were chosen for shade tolerance, mostly, and were held in pots or raised beds. Some of his pots were quite large and expensive to replace, so we took care not to damage them as we moved them from place to place.

The raised beds were bounded by four courses of used railroad ties that gave the area a very urban feel. Amateur came to mind, too, but I don't like that word. People who have credentialed education tend to use it in a derogatory manner when referring to those of us who have no need to be taught how to do what we do. I learned gardening on my own, but I was no amateur. And I wasn't a dabbler. Hiram was.

Still, I didn't care for the use of railroad crossties. They did not fit my personal aesthetic. I also didn't like the positioning of several of the beds. There were five in total but two were used for vegetables, a kind of gardening that did not interest me. So, we eliminated the vegetable beds completely and confined the raised bed feature to one side of the yard

For the beds that remained, we removed the crossties as the border and replaced them with walls made of brick that had been salvaged from an old store in Navasota. We set the brick on a concrete foundation that was eight inches thick and tied the bricks to it with rebar. The bricks were laid in two rows—creating a border with an outer wall and an inner wall that went all the way around each bed—each row about six inches apart with the rebar up the middle between them. For added stability we included a cross-course every four feet, tying the outside row to the inner. When the mortar between the bricks cured, we filled the space between the rows with concrete and added a cap course on top to finish it off. It was more than was required to contain the raised beds, but visitors sometimes like to sit on garden walls. I didn't want these to collapse when they did.

Adding brick walls to contain the raised beds expanded their size—we didn't remove the cross-ties until the brick walls were completed so as to not disturb the plants that were growing there. The sweat and time expended in doing that went a long way toward converting Hiram's back yard into my garden. The transformation took on an additional aspect when I reviewed the plants he'd had placed in the beds.

One bed was filled with nothing but ferns. Another had only caladiums and coleus. The third held impatiens—lots and lots of impatiens. Most people plant impatiens as an annual bedding plant and remove them after they stop blooming. Hiram planted the perennial kind and allowed them to seed. As a result, they returned each year. It was one of the few things that I thought he did correctly, and I liked it. So, I left the impatiens undisturbed.

Rather than trying to continue entirely with shade plants, though, I had a tree service remove the largest tree—an ash that was long past its prime. They also pruned the others to allow more sunlight. Doing that allowed us to change the mix of plants and we added phlox, heliopsis, hosta, and ligularia along with Sweet William, bottle brush buckeye, and a Japanese maple for extra color, especially on the side that did not have the raised beds.

Late that summer, I built a brick wall where the fence between the yards had been. The wall, however, only went part of the way across from either side, leaving an opening in the center for a path. And not a finished wall, either, but one with the middle crumbling down, as if the wall was old, had fallen into disrepair—as if a path opened naturally through a place where the wall had deteriorated. And then I made the path.

While we worked in the garden, a painting crew repainted the house, inside and out, and a contractor added working shutters to all the windows, screened porches to the front and back, and replaced the air conditioner. When the work was completed, I furnished the interior with antiques and collectibles that

I liked, stocked the closets with fresh linens, and dubbed it my guesthouse.

Gradually, the garden became seamless except for the outdoor rooms we'd created with the wall and the raised beds. And slowly, it moved around the ends of the house to overtake the front yard. I helped it by planting ivy on one side and confederate jasmine on the other. After a few seasons, the guesthouse became an ornament in a tangled green morass. For good measure, I added wisteria in two or three places. The lavender flowers in the spring were especially striking.

When I asked Nora Mae what she thought, she said, "You have a guesthouse, but no guests."

And I had an idea for what to do about that.

4

If I had learned anything from my experience in settling Hiram's estate, and in redefining the property that once had been his, it was that meaning and purpose in life come from relationships. Physical objects and professional accomplishments meant very little apart from that. It was my relationship with Hiram that gave meaning to the conversations we shared and the gardening we did together. And it was my relationship with Nora Mae that made our conversations on the back porch meaningful.

If relationships were the key, then repairing relationships was an act of supreme kindness. An act of ultimate purpose and meaning. I knew from my conversations with Nora Mae that her parents were dead and that she and her sisters had not spoken to each other in years. And so, I decided to help Nora Mae repair her relationship with her siblings.

After the two yards were combined into a single garden, the wall constructed, and the house renovated and furnished, I wrote to Nora Mae's sisters—Lucille, Irene, Louise, and Lois—and invited them to celebrate Nora Mae's birthday at my guesthouse. I wasn't sure any of them would respond, much less attend, but a week after I contacted them, Lois accepted my invitation. Louise answered a few days later, followed by Irene after that. Only Lucille was left to respond and when another week went by with no word from her, I telephoned her.

"I received your invitation," Lucille replied when I explained the purpose of my call. "But I'm not interested in Johnny's birthday. And I'm sure as hell not interested in a party for her. She's had parties enough."

"Why do you say that?"

"It's a long story," she said.

"She's your sister," I said.

"That's right." There was a nasty edge to Lucille's voice. "She's my sister, not yours."

"Doesn't that mean something? That she's your sister."

"It meant something to Daddy." The inflection

on that last word spoke volumes. "It doesn't mean much to me."

"Your father cared for her."

"My father cared for all of us."

"But you said, Nora Mae meant something to your father, not to you."

"And?"

"Was there a problem with that?"

"He facilitated her craziness. Look, I'm not comfortable talking about this with a stranger."

I ignored her comment. "He dressed her as a boy."

"Look, after Mama died, things got a little lopsided, if you know what I mean. It was humorous at first, but then it got a little out of hand."

I knew what she was avoiding so I pressed ahead. "In what way?"

"Well, the flat top haircut, for one."

This was a new detail. "He let her get a flattop?" I inflected my voice to sound more surprised than I really was.

"Took her to the barber himself," she announced triumphantly.

"And that was too much for you."

"The jeans. The t-shirts. The caps. All of that was fine," she said. "But the flattop went too far."

"And that happened after your mother died."

"Yes. Once she was gone, there was nothing to curb his need for a boy."

"Nora Mae thinks the reason you won't talk to her is because she had a fling with one of your friends."

"She told you about that?"

"Yes."

"And that's what she thinks this is all about?"

"Isn't it?"

"No," she snapped, and she ended the call abruptly.

Later that day while I was in the garden, my phone rang and I saw from the screen that it was a call from Lucille.

"Look," she began, when I accepted the call. "I'm not angry with you. And I'm not trying to be rude. It's just, there's a lot to this that you don't know and I'm not comfortable talking to you about it. I don't even know you."

"I understand. And my point wasn't to get you to talk to me. I just thought that it would be a tragedy for you all to live your lives and not try to find a way to get along."

"We get along."

"By avoiding each other."

"Well. Yeah."

"Your sisters are coming. And my invitation to you stands. I have plenty of room for all of you in my guesthouse. The five of you can stay over there and shout and yell and argue and say all those things that need to be said."

There was silence for a moment, then she said, "I'll think about it." And she ended the call abruptly once more.

Two weeks before Nora Mae's birthday, I decided I should tell her what I had done. When she came over that afternoon for ginger ale, I told her. She wasn't happy. "This is a big mistake," she said.

"Why?"

"It's too much," she complained.

"Nonsense," I replied. "We'll have the meals catered. And if you decide you want to eat out instead, I'll make the arrangements and cover the cost. It's no trouble at all."

"I didn't mean that."

"Then what did you mean?"

"I mean, too much time has passed. It's too late. And it's none of—"

I cut her off before she could finish. "All of them

are going to be here."

She looked over at me. "All of them?"

"Except for Lucille," I said.

Her shoulders slumped and she looked away. "That figures." There was a note of resignation in her voice.

"What do you mean?"

"Did she tell you why she wasn't coming?"

"She tried."

"Then, I assume she told you it had to do with Daddy and my obsession about being a boy."

"Yes. And his obsession about having a son."

Nora Mae shook her head. "That's what she always says."

"Well," I said with a hopeful tone. "She's not mad about you being with her friend."

Nora Mae frowned. "Her friend?"

"Yeah. In the car. And the boys saw you. And—"

"You talked about that?" Nora Mae's eyes were ablaze.

"I asked her about it. Was I not supposed to?"

"You don't know her. You've never met her." Nora Mae was angry. "And you were talking about the intimate details of my life."

"I'm sorry. I thought—"

"Who else have you told about that?"

"No one." I was feeling defensive. "Why would I talk to anyone else about it?"

"You didn't share it with your buddies down at the café?" Nora Mae had a biting edge to her voice. "Get a good laugh about two lesbians in the back seat, doing the—"

"Stop it," I snapped.

"Just like those boys who saw us that night in the car."

"I haven't told anyone." Now I was angry. "And I only mentioned it to Lucille because you said that's the reason why she was mad at you. But when I asked about why she was mad, she didn't say anything about that incident. She only mentioned the part about you and your father." I sighed and leaned back in the chair. "Come on, Nora Mae. You know me better than this."

"You should stay out of things that don't concern you."

"But this does concern me," I replied.

"I don't think so."

"You're my friend," I insisted. "And this thing with your sisters has gone on long enough. Too long, in fact."

"So, now you're a counselor?" Her voice was heavy with sarcasm.

Condescension always made me angry, but I pushed the feeling aside. “I’ve learned a few things I think can help you.”

Nora Mae stood and handed me her ginger ale bottle. “You need to learn one lesson real good.”

“What’s that?” I asked as I took the bottle from her.

“Stay out of other people’s business.”

And with that, Nora Mae shoved open the screened door, moved quickly down the steps, and disappeared around the end of the house.

Despite the reaction I received from Nora Mae and Lucille, I was determined to follow through with my plan to help the sisters reconcile their differences and restore their relationship. As the date for their arrival drew near, I hired a cleaning crew to make sure the guesthouse was in order, stocked the refrigerator and cabinets with food and drink, and readied my house, just to be prepared.

The event for Nora Mae was scheduled to begin on Friday. The sisters arrived late in the afternoon. Lois and Irene came together. Louise arrived separately. They gathered at my house first and then I rode with them around the block to the guesthouse, which let me know that, in addition to the path I had created between the two properties, I also needed a driveway. Space for that, however, required one of the adjoining houses, of which I made a mental note.

With Irene, Louise, and Lois settled into the guesthouse, I returned home. Nora Mae's absence at the guesthouse had been obvious so I walked across the driveway and knocked her door. She called to me from behind it. "Go away."

"Open the door," I said. "We need to talk."

"I don't want to talk," she replied.

"Your sisters are waiting for you."

"I didn't ask them to come and I don't want to see them."

"They drove here just to celebrate your birthday."

"Not all of them."

"It's a start."

"I appreciate your concern, but I would rather not see them."

"You're treating them rudely," I said. Then I added, "And me, too."

"I didn't ask you to do this."

Rather than argue, I returned home and made coffee, then sat alone at the kitchen table and enjoyed it. Before I finished the first cup, there was a knock at my front door. I thought it might be Nora Mae so I quickly made my way up the hall and looked out a window. Much to my surprise, the person at my front door was Lucille. We had never met but I recognized her from photographs Nora Mae showed me once before.

As I opened the door, Lucille said, "I smell coffee."

"Would you like some?" I asked.

"Please."

She followed me to the kitchen and I gave her a cup, then we walked out to the back porch and sat in the rocking chairs while we drank.

"That's the guesthouse," I said, pointing across the garden. "You can drive around the block and park over there. Or, you can leave your car at the end of the driveway here and walk over."

"Is the guest of honor over there?"

"No," I replied. "I haven't been able to convince her to attend."

"She's angry with us still?"

"She's angry with someone. Me for doing this, I know. I'm not sure why she's angry with y'all."

"I'll talk to her," Lucille offered. "Maybe I can coax her off her high and mighty pedestal." She rose from her chair and pointed. "This is her house over here?"

"Yes," I said.

"Care to join me?"

Given Nora Mae's response to me not quite an hour earlier, I didn't think my presence was a good idea. "Might be better if you go alone," I said.

"Alright." She pushed open the screen door, walked down the steps, and headed across the driveway toward Nora Mae's.

At my usual time, late in the afternoon just as daylight was beginning to wane, I walked out to the porch and sat alone with a bottle of ginger ale in my hand. Two hours had passed since Lucille went over to Nora Mae's house and the thought came to me that perhaps I should check to see if Lucille was safe. I dismissed the notion almost as quickly as it arose, but the idea had traction and didn't quite go away.

A few minutes later, though, I heard them as they came down the driveway and walked past the end of my house. They were chatting and laughing and arm-in-arm and never once looked up to see if I was present. I kept quiet and did nothing to alert them but watched them from my place in the chair on the porch as they made their way up the garden path to the guesthouse and disappeared inside. Through the back window, I saw the sisters cross the room to greet them and they embraced in a group hug. The sight of it left me full and warm inside.

5

The following Tuesday, after Nora Mae's sisters were gone, Nora Mae appeared at my back porch. Mail in hand, she made her way up the steps and took a seat beside me.

"Have a ginger ale," I said.

"Don't mind if I do."

"Lucille and everyone made it home safely, I assume?"

"Yes." Nora Mae reached over and gently rubbed the back of my hand. Our eyes met and she whispered, "Thank you."

"You're very welcome," I replied.

We sat in silence a good long while and watched as the afternoon gently dissolved into twilight. As we were nearing the bottom of the ginger ale bottles,

Nora Mae said, "Lucille was mad at me because I got Mama, and then I got Daddy, and then I got do to whatever I wanted."

"Because your mother died giving birth to you?"

"Yes. And because Daddy dressed me as a boy. I told her he only did that at first. After that, it was my idea. I liked living that way. But it's true, he never made me stop."

"That was when you were a child, too."

"Yes. But she said when I got older and I came out as a lesbian, I got to do that, too."

"Your father didn't try to make you stop?"

Nora Mae shook her head. "He never said a word about it. Never changed the way he treated me. Never said anything about it, one way or the other."

"And Lucille saw that as acceptance."

"It was acceptance. The best kind of acceptance. The kind where you make no judgment about the other person at all."

"And your father never said anything about it?"

"The only thing he said was, 'Nora Mae, if you aren't romantically interested in boys, don't ever let anyone persuade you otherwise. Marriage is a relationship that requires all you have and if you're with a man and you'd rather be with a woman, everyone will be miserable.'"

"Good advice."

"I thought so, too."

"So, Lucille thought you got it all? Your mother, your father, and the life you wanted to live?"

Nora Mae nodded. "She said I got to do everything I ever wanted to do."

"And she didn't?"

"Not in her mind."

"What did she want to do that she didn't get to do?"

"She didn't get to be a ballerina. A professional one."

A frown wrinkled my forehead. "To be what?"

Nora Mae smiled. "Lucille wanted to be a ballerina."

"Why didn't she do it? Even now, it's rather obvious she had the body type for it."

"She had the perfect body for it. And the perfect feet for it, too."

"Then why didn't she?"

"She danced at a small studio in Euless after school. But to be more than that, she needed to go to Dallas and join a professional company. Dallas or Houston. And Daddy wouldn't let her."

"Why not?"

"He thought nothing would come of it."

I shook my head. "How many times have I heard that."

"She's not sad about the way her life turned out," Nora Mae continued. "I mean, it's been a really good life for her. Great husband. Great kids. And life has been good for all of us. But…"

"But none of that speaks to the dream she had."

"Exactly."

"Houston Ballet has a performance every few months," I offered. "I think they have one that starts next week."

"Lucille lives in Dallas."

"Don't they have a ballet company up there?"

"Yes. They do." Nora Mae smiled. "That's why we're meeting up there next weekend to take Lucille to a performance."

My eyes filled with tears at the thought of how things worked together to bring us to that point. Hiram talked to me over the fence. I answered back. We became friends. When he died, he left me his house and all that he owned. Sorting through his belongings brought me to a crisis of meaning and purpose. Found the answer in relationships. Gave away the remainder of his things—most of them—redefined the property that had been his. Infused it with life and purpose once more. Extended that life and purpose to Nora Mae and her sisters. And now they were extending that life to Lucille. It was almost more than I could accept. And the emotion it brought inside me was almost more than I could control.

Nora Mae leaned closer and touched the back of my hand again. "Are you alright?"

"Oh, yes," I whispered. "Quite alright."

We sat in silence again as we emptied the ginger ale bottles and after a while, Nora Mae stood to leave. "You remember what to do?" she asked.

"Pull you out of the house before you stink."

She turned toward the screened door. "Don't forget."

Just as she was about to start down the steps, I said, "Mind if I make a call or two about your trip to Dallas?"

She looked back at me. "What for?"

"I know a couple of people with connections to the arts in Dallas. They might be able to get you backstage."

Nora Mae grinned. "That would be wonderful."

FICTION BY JOE HILLEY

THE MIKE CONNOLLY MYSTERY SERIES:

Sober Justice

Double Take

Night Rain

Electric Beach

The Deposition

Sunset Motel

GENERAL FICTION:

What the Red Moon Knows

The Art Dealer's Wife

SHORT STORY COLLECTIONS:

The Legend of Dell Briggers

Other People, Other Places

For more information visit Joe's website:
JoeHilley.com